CRITICAL RESPONSE

A CHRISTIAN ROMANTIC SUSPENSE

FINNEGAN FIRST RESPONDERS

LAURA SCOTT

CHAPTER ONE

———————

"Alanna, you're up for the ambo patient slotted for room three."

Alanna Finnegan nodded to indicate she'd heard the charge nurse's directive as she finished typing her discharge note. No surprise that she'd discharged one patient barely two minutes ago and the next one was already on the way. Beds in the emergency department rarely grew cold between patients. October wasn't as busy as summertime, but the nice weather had lingered, keeping the influx of patients steady.

In truth, she'd rather be busy during her long twelve-hour shifts.

One thing was for sure, this job was never boring. Her feet ached from the miles she put on every shift, but she didn't mind. After finishing at the computer, she stood and glanced up at the census board. Now that the hospital's medical records were computerized, names of their incoming patients automatically populated the screen thanks to the dispatcher working in the paramedic base. Her new admission was a twenty-three-year-old man named Ivan Garcia. And no surprise, his presenting problem was a gunshot wound to the thigh.

Trinity Medical Center was the only level one trauma center in the city of Milwaukee. The nursing staff with their gallows humor described those patients with gunshot or knife wounds as injuries as kids playing in the knife and gun club. Not that the injuries were always their fault, innocent people could be victims of crimes. But she had enough experience to know the innocent victims were in the less than 15 percent category. The other 85 percent were generally not so innocent and therefore were accompanied by Milwaukee police officers when they were injured during the commission of a crime.

Ivan's injury must not be serious enough to require a trip to the trauma bay. Her patient would be there at any moment, so she peeked inside to make sure the room had been cleaned. Karin Graves, their housekeeper, was good about being on top of things. Thankfully, she'd been in and out in record time, and the room sparkled. Since she wasn't sure if the patient's bullet would need to be removed, she set up a surgical tray on a table in the corner near the doorway, just in case. She deftly unwrapped the tray, while leaving the clear plastic covering to keep the instruments sterile while being readily accessible.

Thirty seconds later, the ambulance bay doors burst open. Two EMTs wheeled a gurney through the opening. No police officer was in attendance, indicating the patient was not in custody. Which was probably a good thing. It didn't really matter to her one way or the other, she treated her patients equally regardless of their guilt or innocence.

"Twenty-three-year-old male suffering a gunshot wound to the right thigh. His vitals are stable," the female paramedic said as they pushed the gurney into the room.

"Bullet is still embedded in the thigh muscle; we've packed the wound with gauze."

"Thanks." Together, they moved Ivan Garcia from the ambulance gurney to the bed using the sheet beneath him to slide him over. The EMTs wheeled the cart out of the room, drawing the privacy curtain closed behind them. Their job of transporting the patient was over.

This young man was her patient now. She smiled down at him as she pulled her stethoscope from around her neck. Even though there were no police officers in attendance, she couldn't help noticing the three red teardrops tattooed down his face from the corner of his right eye. She knew gangs used that tattoo to boast about killing people, one teardrop for each person. Three in Ivan's case. Averting her gaze, she reminded herself that this guy was twenty-three. He could have done the deed years ago; she'd seen similar tattoos on fifteen-year-old kids. "Ivan, my name is Alanna. I'll be your nurse for the next two hours." Her shift officially ended at seven thirty in the evening, but she often had to stay later to help keep the patients flowing in and out of the department. "How are you feeling?"

"How do you think?" Ivan scowled. "I've been shot."

She nodded, her gaze sympathetic. "I know. How is your thigh pain?"

"Bad." He pinned her with a narrow gaze. "Ten out of ten." The way he'd used the pain score of ten out of ten indicated he was no stranger to being in the hospital. Had he been admitted with other injuries? Maybe those red teardrops had been inked on his skin more recently than she'd thought. A twinge of unease niggled at the back of her neck. She did her best to ignore it.

"Okay, I'll ask the doctor if he'll order you some pain medication. First, though, I need to listen to your heart and lungs and take a set of vital signs." His heartbeat was strong, his lungs clear. She took his blood pressure, noting the higher reading likely due to his pain, then removed the cuff from his arm. "We need to have you connected to our heart monitor, okay?"

She turned to grab the EKG patches from the package behind her, intending to place them on his chest. Before she could do anything, her patient abruptly rolled off the gurney and grabbed her from behind. He brought his arm across her neck, pressing tightly against her throat in a vice-like grip.

She was so surprised by his actions she didn't have time to scream. With his arm choking her, breathing was impossible too.

Help, she silently shouted.

"You're going to get me outta here before the cops show up, understand?" The harsh voice in her ear was punctuated by a tightening of his arm around her neck. This close, he reeked of sweat and alcohol. Anxious to appease him, she nodded.

Ivan dragged her several feet across the room before she could get her bearings. No! This couldn't be happening! Remembering his thigh wound, she tried to wiggle into a better position to use his injury to escape.

She hadn't grown up with six older brothers without learning some self-defense.

Ivan stopped near the curtain as if understanding there would be plenty of other staff members outside the room. She used his momentary pause to her advantage, lifting her right leg and kicking backward at his injured thigh and knee with all her strength. Her rubber-soled shoes wouldn't normally do much damage, but somehow she managed to hit her target.

Ivan sucked in a harsh breath at the pain but didn't scream or cry out. His grip around her neck tightened painfully, choking her. He reached out toward the surgical tray and poked his fingers through the plastic to grab the scalpel. "Do that again and I'll slice your throat, understand?" His voice was low and harsh in her ear. She could smell his foul breath and tried not to gag. "I'm not going back to jail!"

Alanna froze when the sharp edge of the blade cut into the skin beneath her chin. Warm blood trickled down her neck, running over his arm still locked around her throat.

Why had she set up the surgical tray? She inwardly railed at herself for being so foolish, even though it was too late for regrets now.

"We're walking out of here." He twisted his body to use his shoulder to shove the privacy curtain aside. He dragged her through the opening, and at first, no one paid them any attention.

People came in and out of rooms all the time. She tried to call out but could only make a croaking sound.

One of her nurse colleagues, Dana Callahan, glanced over. Her eyes widened when she saw the arm across Alanna's throat and the blood staining her neck. "Hey, what are you doing?"

"Stay back or I'll kill her!" Ivan's voice echoed through the area. The ED was set up in teams of rooms, and they were in the orange team, which was closest to the red team formerly known as the trauma bay.

Dana's, Dr. Willis's, and even the housekeeper Karin's expressions all reflected surprise and horror. They simply stood there, gaping in shock as Ivan held the blade to her throat. She couldn't really blame them. She doubted she'd have reacted much differently.

Alanna wanted to kick at Ivan's injured leg again but feared the blade of the scalpel was too close to her jugular vein, or worse, her carotid artery. One deep swipe and she could easily bleed out before anyone could save her.

Please, Lord Jesus, keep us all safe!

A sense of calmness washed over her. Ivan wanted her for a reason. His plan was to escape being questioned by the police. All gunshot and knife wounds were an automatic report to the cops. By playing along, she could buy time.

There was a Milwaukee County sheriff's deputy stationed in the waiting room of the emergency department to help deal with family members of patients who were in police custody. An unfortunately common occurrence. Someone would call him or her in to help.

Her patient continued dragging her step by step toward the ambulance bay doors. Her ID badge was dislodged from her scrubs and dropped to the floor, the hard plastic making a soft noise as it hit the linoleum and skated across the floor.

"Hey, you need to let Alanna go." Doctor Willis, the attending physician assigned to the orange team, stepped forward, concern etched in his features. "You want to leave without receiving medical care and treatment? That's fine with us. But kidnapping a staff member is going to bring all kinds of trouble raining down on you."

"Stay back!" Ivan shouted, dragging her closer to the ambulance bay doors. "I swear I'll kill her!"

Alanna wanted to believe it was an empty threat, but the sharp edge of the blade convinced her otherwise. The three red teardrops inked on his face flashed in her memory. He'd killed before, and she knew he wouldn't hesitate to kill again. She tried to swallow past the forearm pressed against her throat. Her inability to breathe normally was making her dizzy.

How long before she passed out?

Not long.

Her foot tangled with the legs of a chair as Ivan continued dragging her past the row of rooms. She gripped his arm to keep herself from falling. The blade dug deeper into her neck. Tears pricked her eyes as she struggled to stay upright and focused. Surely, he'd let her go once they were outside.

And if he didn't?

He could take her with him, or simply kill her.

Her gaze stumbled across a tall dark-haired man wearing a police uniform moving between the staff members. She recognized him as MPD Officer Reed Carmichael. He worked out of the Fifth Precinct and often accompanied patients to the emergency department. Had, in fact, done that very thing last week during their respective shifts.

His blue eyes were locked on hers as he edged closer, using the staff as camouflage. His gaze silently promised he was there to rescue her.

Looking into Reed's calm eyes made her relax. She'd gotten to know him over the busy summer months and trusted him almost as much as she did her cop brothers.

"Stop where you are, pig!" Ivan shouted. "One step closer and I'll slice her throat."

Reed stopped halfway behind Dr. Willis. Alanna had hoped Ivan wouldn't notice Reed's approach, but the guy's survival instincts had been honed to a sharp edge, much like the scalpel at her neck.

Ivan pulled her closer to the ambulance bay doors, leaving her little choice but to go along with him. She'd hoped he would let her go once they were outside, but she wasn't sure that was Ivan's intent at all.

The ambulance doors opened, and two more men stepped through the doorway. She couldn't see them clearly but heard Ivan's grunt as if he'd expected to have assistance.

No! They were going to kidnap her!

A gunshot rang out. The arm around her throat loosened. She gasped for breath, dropping to the floor as Ivan's body fell backward. Blood ran freely down her neck from where the scalpel blade had sliced along her skin.

"Alanna!" Her name was a strangled sound as Reed ran toward her. She stared up at him for a second before everything went dark.

———

"WHERE'S THE DOC?" Reed Carmichael cradled Alanna Finnegan in his arms on the floor, glancing frantically toward the hospital staff. "Her throat has been cut!"

A physician and a dark-haired nurse named Dana came running over. The doc's expression turned grim. "I don't think he hit the artery, but we need to get her into room three."

Knowing the general layout of the emergency department, Reed didn't hesitate to scoop Alanna into his arms. He strode to room three. The bed was messy, making him realize this must have been the room the perp had been in. It wasn't ideal, but this was likely the only empty room they had. He gently set her on the bed, then forced himself to step back, giving Dana and the doc room to work.

Reed's heart thumped against his ribs as the medical team tended to Alanna. She was in good hands, so he turned away to head back over to where Ivan Garcia, a.k.a. Ice, was lying dead on the hospital floor. There was blood everywhere, Alanna's and Ivan's. Mostly Ivan's. He glanced toward the ambulance doors, but the two men who'd come through earlier were gone now. As much as he wanted to track them down, he couldn't leave the scene of an officer-involved shooting.

Especially when he was the officer involved.

Taking out a perp was bad enough, but doing so in the middle of a hospital emergency department was worse. He could already hear the MPD upper brass and hospital administrators screaming about this.

And he understood this never should have happened. Where in the world was Wesley Durango? His rookie partner was supposed to accompany Ice to the hospital. The shooting scene where two rival gangs had fought had been chaotic, but he'd thought the rookie had jumped up into the ambulance with their wounded perp, the way he'd told him to.

Yet if he had, there was no sign of Durango now.

Reed half expected the rookie to have gone to find a cup of coffee or something as equally ridiculous. Yet that didn't change the fact that Durango should have had Ivan Garcia cuffed to the bed. And the rookie should have never left Garcia's side.

Sheriff's Deputy Mike Callahan came rushing in from the waiting room, accompanied by a woman in a suit, clearly someone from the C suite. "What happened?" Mike asked.

Reed glanced at the hospital administrator. Her name badge identified her as Kathy Tusk, Vice President of Hospital Operations.

This was the beginning of his interrogation, one that would start with the hospital administrators and continue through the internal affairs division of the Milwaukee Police Department. He gestured toward the dead man.

"This is Ivan Garcia, a.k.a. Ice. He's a member of the Blood Kings, a well-known drug-and-gun-running gang."

"You shot him in the hospital?" Tusk demanded harshly. "What were you thinking?"

"He held your nurse hostage with a scalpel blade to her neck. I had to stop him before he dragged her from the building." He glanced at Mike Callahan. "There were two other gang members who came in through the ambulance doors, so I feared the worst. But they left when I took out Garcia. We need all the video surveillance of the incident so we can get their pictures out to every cop on the street."

"You'll need a warrant to get the video," Tusk snapped.

Reed tamped down his anger. This woman acted as if she was more concerned about his shooting of a gang member than she was about her own staff member. "I'm sure you'll want to check in on Alanna Finnegan. She's being treated for her neck wound in room 3."

Tusk paled and spun away to see for herself. Mike sent him a sympathetic glance. "Have you called this in?"

"Not yet." He lifted his hand to his radio to make the call. The minute he said the words officer-involved shooting, he'd heard the dispatcher suck in a harsh breath and knew there would be dozens of cops on campus within minutes. He released the radio and sighed. "The worst part is that I'll be placed on administrative leave."

"I know. That's a bummer." Mike clapped him on the shoulder. "Good shooting, though. I'm glad you saved my cousin's life."

"Your cousin?" He glanced back toward Alanna's room. "I didn't realize you were related."

"We only found out earlier this year. And technically, we're second cousins." Mike's expression turned serious.

"That was a close call. How did Ice get a weapon in the first place?"

"It must have been in the room. I'm sure there are plenty of scalpels and other sharp objects here that can be turned against the staff." Reed rubbed the back of his neck, feeling the weight of his actions bearing down on him. The upper brass would watch whatever video was available and interview witnesses, dissecting everything he'd done or hadn't done. It was difficult to make administrators understand how fast a situation could unravel.

The second he'd seen the two additional gang members coming inside, he'd been forced to use deadly force to save Alanna's life. The three of them would have gotten her outside if he hadn't. And he'd had a feeling, deep in his bones, that they'd planned to kill her.

He walked back toward Alanna's room. Her eyes were open now, and there was a gauze bandage over the cut in her throat. The doc was explaining about the stitches that would need to be placed to close the wound, reassuring her that they'd have a plastic surgeon do the work to minimize a scar.

Alanna's gaze shifted from the doctor to him. Her dark-brown eyes shone with gratitude as they clung to his. He wanted to push past everyone to reach her bedside and take her hand. To assure her she'd never be hurt like that again.

But he didn't. Pounding footsteps indicated his backup had arrived. He turned to see several cops rushing in through the ambulance bay doors, stopping abruptly upon seeing the perp lying dead on the floor.

Yeah, this would be a mess. When Sergeant Noah Sinclair walked in, he headed straight toward him. He offered his weapon, butt first, then unclipped his badge and handed that over as well. Sinclair took both items, dropping them into an evidence bag.

"What happened?" Noah Sinclair was known to be a fair and decent boss. He didn't sit behind the desk like some of the older guys, preferring being out in the field. Reed also knew Noah was Mike Callahan's brother-in-law; he was married to Maddy who worked for the DA's office. Reed and other officers often had to testify in court for the prosecutor related to criminal activities.

Reed was surprised to note that the rookie wasn't among those who'd come rushing to the hospital. Where was he? He turned his attention to Noah. "I take full responsibility, Sarg. I asked my partner, Wes, to accompany this perp to the emergency department, but he must not have followed through. The perp wasn't cuffed to the bed." He and several other cops had been dealing with rival gang members, who had been armed.

Noah grimaced but nodded. "I'll talk to him. What happened here?"

Reed filled him in on how Ivan "Ice" Garcia had taken Alanna as a hostage by holding a scalpel to her neck. "I don't know what he intended, but it could be that he wanted her to provide medical care to his gunshot wound outside the hospital."

"Alanna Finnegan?" Noah sighed. "Great, we'll be hearing from her brothers Rhy and Tarin any minute."

"I know." The Finnegan family had gotten some press over the past several months, especially with Tarin being a detective and Rhy being captain of the tactical unit. Alanna had mentioned her family during one of their brief conversations. And now he could add the Callahans into the mix. As if having siblings in law enforcement wasn't enough, there were cousins too. "Ice was dragging Alanna toward the door. When two gang members showed up, I had little choice but to shoot him, taking him out of the picture to save Alanna's life. Unfortunately, that sent the other gang members running. We may get something off the hospital video on their ride, which could lead us to them."

"Do you think they wanted something more than nursing care from Alanna?" Noah asked.

He shrugged. "Anything is possible, but how would Ice know Alanna would be assigned as his nurse? At the most, he may have known she was working today, but even that wouldn't be easy to find out. Not unless he knew someone working inside the hospital. Besides, I don't think he'd shoot himself on purpose to get here." The more he thought about it, the less he believed this to be a personal attack against Alanna. "I was on scene when the drug deal went south. Ice was shot by a rival gang member from the Latino Hombres. I think his grabbing Alanna had been a spur-of-the-moment decision. Maybe an attempt to avoid jail time."

"Yeah, okay." Noah glanced around at the chaotic scene in the emergency department. "This will be a nightmare."

"Tell me about it." Reed didn't think there was anything he could have done differently. Other than making sure his rookie partner had done his job in accompanying Ice to the hospital.

The rookie's absence concerned him. "Sarg, I haven't seen Wes Durango since we responded to the scene of the initial shooting. As far as I know, he hasn't shown up here yet."

Noah's scowl deepened as he used his radio to contact the rookie. There was a long pause as Sinclair waited.

No response.

A shiver of unease slid down his spine. Without hesitation, Reed ran through the ambulance bay doors and into the cool autumn air. He took his time searching each of the squads that were parked all along the front of the emergency department.

Where was the rookie?

Reed's gaze dropped to the squad he'd driven here. He'd purposefully left it parked near the multilevel concrete parking garage. He frowned when he noticed someone was in the passenger seat.

Wesley? That was odd because Reed had come here alone, having assumed—apparently wrongly—that his partner was with Ice at the hospital.

He jogged over to the squad, his stomach knotting painfully. Someone was sitting inside, head resting against the passenger-side window as if taking a nap. The guy had light hair, much like Wesley's, but he couldn't see his face clearly to make a positive identification.

It was hard to imagine the rookie would risk sleeping on the job. He may not have done everything the way he should have, but even he wouldn't be that clueless.

As he opened the door, the person inside toppled out of the squad, hitting the asphalt road with a hard thud. The rookie's pale-white face pointed to the sky.

And above his dead stare was a small, round bullet hole.

Wesley Durango had been murdered!

CHAPTER TWO

Alanna would have preferred taking care of three rambunctious patients at once rather than lying still while a plastic surgery resident stitched the wound in her neck. She didn't much care for being on this end of the hospital bed.

It was humiliating to realize she'd passed out after Reed shot her patient. Something she'd never done before. Not even during her nursing training when she'd taken care of some grisly wounds involving blood, brain matter, and amputated extremities. With eight siblings, all but one older than her, she'd considered herself to be tough.

Apparently, she was a marshmallow. Collapsing like a damsel in distress. How embarrassing.

She owed Reed Carmichael for saving her life. The moment she'd glimpsed him moving through the emergency department, she'd known he would do everything possible to rescue her. Yet she wished he hadn't needed to use lethal force. She could only imagine what he was going through. She knew from her older cop brothers that Reed would be put on administrative leave until his actions had been thoroughly investigated.

"All done," the resident said with a smile.

"Thanks." She could feel the tightness where he'd placed the sutures. The incision would hurt like crazy once the local anesthetic wore off. When the resident turned to leave, she sat up on the edge of the bed.

"Alanna!" Rhy bulldozed past the resident to enter the room, his brow creased with worry. "Are you okay?"

She should have known her eldest brother would have heard about this through the police grapevine. She managed a smile. "I'm fine, Rhy. How are you? And Devon? Is she feeling okay? How's the baby?"

"She wasn't the one held hostage," Rhy shot back. Then he amended, "Devon is fine. Anxious for the baby to be born next month."

"Great." She groaned when Tarin came in. "Please tell me you didn't bring the entire family here. Not for something this minor. It's just a few stitches."

"We didn't bring the entire family, although you should have called us to let us know what was going on." Tarin's gaze zeroed in on the narrow line of sutures. "How many?"

"Only ten," she hastened to reassure them. Rhy and Tarin were the oldest of the nine Finnegan siblings. They'd stepped up to hold the family together after their parents had died in a car crash over ten years ago. She and her twin Aiden had been seventeen at the time, and Elly, the youngest, was only fourteen. Alanna admired her oldest siblings, but she knew they were overreacting by rushing to the hospital to see her. She suspected part of the reason they'd come was to learn more about how the event had unfolded. "I would have called, but I've been busy. Don't worry, I'm fine. Thanks to Officer Reed Carmichael."

Rhy and Tarin exchanged a long glance. "We heard from both Mike Callahan and Sergeant Noah Sinclair about how Carmichael took the perp down," Rhy said. "But what we don't understand is why this guy wasn't in police custody. He should have been cuffed to the bed with an officer standing guard."

Since she had no idea why Ivan Garcia hadn't been accompanied by the police, she didn't comment. "I'm sure that will be part of the investigation."

"It better be," Rhy muttered darkly. He ran his fingers over his short blond hair. "This was a close one, sis. It could have ended badly."

"I'm aware." She strove to keep her tone light. "You know as well as I do that God was watching out for me."

"He was," Tarin murmured in agreement.

"Look, will you please let the rest of the family know I'm fine?" Alanna glanced at each of her brothers. "Especially Aiden, as I know he's training this weekend. I don't want him to come rushing home for no reason." Her twin, Aiden, was with the National Guard. They'd often fought as kids, but Aiden had also taken on the role of her protector. Especially during high school and college.

"Okay, but let me know when you're ready to go," Rhy said. "I'll take you back to the homestead."

The family home in Brookland had been dubbed the homestead by their parents, and the name had stuck over the years. Alanna loved the big six-bedroom house where she'd grown up and had lived until a few months ago. But she liked being independent and had no intention of going with Rhy, who took his role as head of the household very seriously. "I have my car here. I'd rather go home. I'm tired and sore. What I really need is peace and quiet."

Rhy's scowl deepened. "We'll take care of you."

"I'm fine." She managed a reassuring smile. "I have the next two days off, which will help."

"I'm sure she'll be okay." Surprisingly, Tarin came to her defense. "The homestead is not known for peace and quiet."

"Like it's my fault there are people coming and going at all times?" Rhy's tone betrayed a hint of frustration. "It's not like we have a full house."

"You, Devon, Elly, Aiden, Colin, and Faye." Tarin ticked the family members off on his fingers. "That's six, although I will concede that Aiden is out of town at training."

"Colin and Faye are moving into their own place by the end of the month," Rhy pointed out. He held her gaze for a long moment, then shrugged. "Okay, fine. But I want you to promise to call if you need something."

"I will." She sent Tarin a thankful look.

Her brothers left, no doubt planning to talk to the officers still on scene about what had transpired. She barely had time to relax when Dana Callahan rushed into the room.

"How are you feeling?" Dana raked a critical eye over her. "Are you okay?"

"I'm fine." She proved her point by sliding off the bed to stand on her own two feet. Thankfully, the room didn't spin. "I'm surprised you're still here. Isn't our shift over?"

"It's chaos out there," Dana confided. "They finally moved the dead guy to the morgue, but there are cops everywhere, including your brothers and my brother-in-law. And the hospital administrators are here too. I've never seen so many suits in one place in my life."

She could imagine how upset hospital management must be over the shooting that had taken place in their emergency department. The thought of dealing with them made her headache worse. "I was hoping to head home."

"You should. Didn't the VP of operations already take your statement?"

"Yes." At least that interaction hadn't been too bad. And it had been cut short by the arrival of the plastic surgery resident. The VP had looked a bit pale at seeing her incision, which had given Alanna a flash of satisfaction. Easy to sit in C-suite offices all day making decisions that impacted the front line, but seeing firsthand what it was like working in the ED was something very different. She was glad the woman had gotten a glimpse of reality.

Dana frowned. "Hey, where is your ID badge? You can't clock out at the end of your shift or get your car out of the parking structure without it."

Alanna put her hand up to the V-neck of her scrub top, swallowing hard as she relived those moments when she'd been dragged through the department. "I think it fell off."

"Stay here, I'll go look for it. Oh, and you need to take clear bandages with you to place over the sutures while you shower." Dana gently pushed her toward a chair. "Please sit. I'll get what you need. You don't look so good."

She didn't feel good either, so she dropped into the chair. If Dana couldn't find her ID badge, she'd need to go to security to get another one. Hopefully, they wouldn't make her take another photo. She put a hand to her hair, wincing when she realized there was dried blood stuck to the blond strands.

Her blood? Or Ivan Garcia's? Her stomach somersaulted at the possibility of the latter.

After a few minutes, Dana poked her head in the room. "Alanna? I have Calvin Richter from security bringing you a new ID. There's no sign of your badge anywhere; we think the police may have taken it."

She inwardly groaned. "Okay. I hope he hurries."

"He will." She came into the room with a handful of clear plastic dressings. "Take these. I'll finish your note on Garcia."

"No, I'll do it." Alanna set the dressings aside. She hadn't even thought about the fact that she needed to complete a discharge note on her patient. And what exactly would she write? His dragging her out of the room with a blade to her throat didn't belong in his medical record.

Since she had to wait for Calvin anyway, she rose and crossed over to the computer. She logged in manually since she couldn't use her ID badge and opened Ivan Garcia's chart. She quickly typed in the brief exam and his blood pressure reading she'd gotten. She held her fingers over the keyboard, trying to think of a way to professionally end the note. Finally, she typed a brief statement.

Patient left without receiving any medical or nursing care.

It was true, and everything Ivan Garcia did after leaving the room would have to be entered into the hospital incident reporting system, not his medical record. She sighed, realizing she'd have to be the one to do that report. She quickly did so, deciding to get it over with. When that task was finished, she logged off.

"Ms. Alanna?" Calvin hovered in the doorway, and just seeing him made her smile. Calvin Richter was old enough to be her father, and his long tenure as a hospital security guard made him a favorite among the staff. "I have your replacement ID badge."

"Thanks, Calvin." She scooped up the clear bandages Dana had brought for her, then crossed over to take the card from him. It was difficult to get anywhere in the facility without having her badge to access secured doorways. "I appreciate you making a new one so quickly."

"I hope you're doing okay." His brow furrowed. "I saw what happened on the video monitor."

"I'm fine." It was disconcerting to think about how many people had watched the video and how many more would continue to do so over the next few days. She was never one to seek the spotlight but had a feeling she'd be well known throughout the entire medical center after this. "I'm just anxious to get home."

"I'll escort you to your car," he offered.

"Thanks." She told herself she wasn't being a marshmallow by taking Calvin up on his offer. She wasn't badly hurt, but being threatened by a patient holding a blade to her throat was hardly an everyday occurrence.

There was no doubt in her mind that Ivan Garcia would have slit her throat without a second thought. Adding another red-inked teardrop tattoo to his face. Thanks to Reed, Ivan would never hurt anyone ever again.

Stepping through the doorway, she moved across the door and into the main emergency department. Chaotic was putting it mildly; there were dozens of cops and suits milling about. She tried to find Reed, hoping to thank him, but she didn't see him.

"I, uh, need to get my purse out of my locker." When Calvin nodded in understanding, she turned to head in the opposite direction from the large cluster of people. It didn't take long to use her new badge to unlock the nurses' locker room door and then to grab her purse from her locker. She tucked the dressings inside and clipped her ID badge to her collar. "Okay, I'm ready."

Calvin escorted her outside through the main doors. There were dozens of squads parked in the semicircle driveway, and she wondered how many patients had dared come through the gauntlet of police to seek care. Many, she knew, avoided the police.

Her gaze landed on a cop sitting on the curb, holding his head in his hands. Reed? She quickly hurried over to drop down beside him, resting her hand on his back. "Are you okay?"

"Alanna?" His head lifted, his gaze meeting hers. "You're leaving?"

"My shift ended an hour ago, and I've been cleared to leave." The darkness made it difficult to read his expression. "I'm sorry you're in the hot seat. I hope it doesn't take them too long to finish the investigation."

"It doesn't matter. I'd do it again in a heartbeat." He rose to his feet, then offered her his hand. Her palm tingled as he gently pulled her upright. "Come on, I'll walk you to your car."

"Oh, I—uh." She glanced over to see Calvin had taken several steps backward, a knowing grin on his features. He waved his hand, indicating she should go ahead, then turned to head back inside.

Was Calvin playing matchmaker now? Swallowing a sigh, she faced Reed and nodded. "Thanks, I'd appreciate that."

It didn't matter who walked her to her car. The sooner she made it home, the better.

She'd had enough drama for one day.

SEEING Alanna had given him a boost of energy. Something he'd badly needed since his partner's dead body had fallen out of their squad. If not for the video feed showing two men in hoodies shoving the dead cop inside, Reed suspected he'd be in jail for the rookie's murder.

"Will you give me a minute?" He put a hand on Alanna's arm. "I need to let the upper brass know I'm leaving."

"Sure."

Reed strode toward the group of cops clustered around his squad. They'd removed Wesley's body, but the vehicle itself would be combed for evidence. Per the video, the hoodie guys were wearing masks and gloves, but there was the possibility of hair samples being left behind.

Not that he held out much hope they'd find anything useful. The way the hooded suspects had stuffed Wesley's body inside the squad had reeked of brazen confidence.

He felt certain they were members of the Blood Kings, but without proof, there was nothing he or those officers assigned to the scene could do about it.

"I'm leaving," Reed said bluntly. This shooting was a big deal; Adams rarely showed up on scene. And his boss had been at the shooting scene earlier too. Busy day for the captain. "You know where to find me if you have more questions."

"Fine." Captain Jake Adams glared at him as if the rookie's murder was his fault. And maybe it was. He'd been torturing himself over the past few hours about what he could have done differently.

Without saying anything more, Reed turned away. Seeing Alanna waiting for him gave him a sense of peace. Maybe he'd done some things wrong, but he did not regret taking down Ivan Garcia. He managed a smile, placing his hand on her back to urge her forward. "I have a favor to ask in return."

"What's that?" She cast him a sideways glance as they walked toward the staff parking structure.

"Would you mind if I bum a ride to your place? From there, I can get a rideshare home." He didn't relish the idea of calling a rideshare to the sea of cops staked out at the entrance to the emergency department.

"I'll drive you home." She frowned. "I assume you drove here, right? They won't even let you take the squad to get home?"

"No." Reed grimaced. "Unfortunately, the squad is a crime scene."

"What?" She abruptly stopped to gape at him. "I don't understand. I thought the crime scene was inside the emergency department."

"I'll explain on the way." He wouldn't be able to tell her too much in case the investigation done by the internal affairs department didn't go well.

She dug in her purse for her keys, then continued toward the parking structure. "I'm on the third level."

"Let's take the elevator." To his nonmedical eye, she looked pale and tired. The row of stitches marred her beautiful skin, but he knew the injury could have been much worse. She normally wore her long blond hair back at work, but strands fell around her face, revealing clumps of dried blood.

When they reached her car, he held out his hand for the keys. "Why don't you let me drive?"

A frown puckered her brow. "It's my car."

"I know, but you look exhausted. It's been a long day."

"For you too." She hesitated, then dropped the key fob into his palm. "Okay, but drive to your place. I'll head home from there."

He opened the passenger-side door for her, then went around to slide in behind the wheel. "Where do you live? Close to the hospital?"

"Yes." She clasped her seat belt, then rested her head against the cushion. "My condo is only a mile away, west of the hospital. I should walk to work, but after being on my feet for twelve and a half hours or more, I can't bear the thought of walking another mile to get home. Especially at night."

The neighborhood around the medical center was safe enough, but he understood her concern. A beautiful woman like Alanna needed to be careful.

He drove out of the parking structure, pausing at the gate. Alanna passed her ID badge over so he could scan it to get through. When the gate lifted, he drove out, handing the badge back to her.

"How far away to you live?" She tucked the badge in her purse. "I really think you should drive to your place, Reed. I'm perfectly capable of driving myself home."

He hesitated, then nodded. "I own a small house that isn't too far from your condo. You're across the street from the Irish Pub, right?"

"Right." The corner of her mouth tipped up in a weak smile. "I may have been there a few times."

"Me too." He turned west, heading to her condo. "I'll drive you home. I can walk to my place from there. It's only another eight blocks or so."

"Okay."

Reed was glad she'd accepted his compromise. As he drove toward her condo building, the shooting event that had sparked all of this flashed in his mind. A dispute between the Blood Kings and Latino Hombres had started this mess.

But why had his rookie partner, Wesley Durango, been murdered? Killing a cop made no sense. Any gang banger knew that killing a cop was asking for trouble. The entire police department wouldn't rest until they found the man responsible.

Was that the motive? Did one gang member kill Wesley to frame their rival gang?

"You look so serious," Alanna murmured. "I feel terrible that you've been placed on administrative leave over saving my life."

"I told you I would do it again in a heartbeat." He surprised himself by reaching over to take her hand. "I was terrified he'd kill you. I had to act fast; there was no time to waste when Ivan's gang-banger buddies arrived."

"I heard someone coming in through the ambo doors and feared the worst." She clung to his hand. "What did you mean about your squad being a crime scene?"

He hesitated. How much could he say? "There was another murder near my squad."

"Another murder?" Alanna's fingers tightened around his as she sat up straighter in her seat. "Who?"

"I'm sorry, but I can't talk about it." That he even wanted to surprised him. "I will tell you that the murder is likely related to the gang member who held you hostage."

"So that's why there were so many cops there." She shook her head. "Wow. I can't believe this is happening."

"I know what you mean." He hadn't expected to be smack in the middle of this mess either. "I saw your brothers Rhy and Tarin. I'm surprised you didn't leave with them."

"Oh, Rhy tried to make me go with him back to the homestead, but I refused. I love my family, but they can be overbearing at times."

"I can only imagine." He knew she had eight siblings, one of them being her twin. "But you shouldn't be alone either. You might have nightmares."

"I'll be fine." He didn't like the way she brushed off his

concern. Suffering post-traumatic stress wasn't something to take lightly.

"Would you do me a favor?" Alanna asked.

"Of course." He glanced at her. "What do you need?"

"This might sound silly, but would you mind driving past your house so I can see where you live?"

"I can do that." He wondered if she was having second thoughts about being home alone. Spending a few extra minutes with her was no hardship, so he turned onto the next street after passing her condo building to head to his place.

He lived in a small blue Cape Cod–style house. It only had two bedrooms as the previous owner had taken down a wall to make one larger master suite. As the house was within his budget, the lack of a third bedroom hadn't bothered him.

"Did you think I was lying about where I lived?" He pulled up in front of his house and gestured at it. "It may not be much, but I like it."

"No, I didn't think you were lying, and it's a very cute place." Alanna smiled with appreciation. "It is within walking distance too." She turned to face him. "How is it that we didn't know how close we lived to each other until now?"

"I have no idea." He'd been tempted to ask her out last week when he'd had a prisoner patient in the ED, but the timing hadn't seemed right. Flirting while on the job wasn't smart. Besides, he'd been burned in the past by a fellow female officer and wasn't sure he was ready to try the dating scene again. He began pulling away from the curb when he noticed a car without headlights coming up fast behind them.

Alarm skittered along his nerves. He punched the gas,

sending them lurching forward. Alanna grabbed her armrest as he continued pressing down on the accelerator.

"What's wrong?" She twisted in her seat. "Who's back there?"

"I don't know. Hang on." He made a sharp turn up the cross street, driving as fast as he dared through the suburban neighborhood while keeping a wary eye on the rearview mirror. The car driving without headlights indicated they were looking for trouble. When he caught a glimpse of a dark car turning the corner behind him, he wrenched the wheel to make another turn. He had a bad feeling about who was in the car behind them. "Call 911!"

"Okay." She fumbled with her phone as he continued driving erratically through the neighborhood that he thankfully knew very well. As a runner, he routinely took different paths each morning before hitting the Oak Leaf Trail.

Reed thought for sure he'd lost the vehicle following them when a dark shape passed beneath a streetlight. Tense with frustration, he stomped on the gas again, trying to pull away. But he wasn't fast enough.

Gunfire rang out, shattering the rear window of Alanna's sedan. "Get down," he shouted hoarsely.

Alanna ducked in the seat beside him but continued updating the dispatcher on the situation with an eerie calmness, one born from years of working under pressure in the busiest emergency department in the city.

It wasn't until the shrill sirens of a multi-squad police response filled the night air that the dark car behind him abruptly turned away. He watched through the rearview mirror as the vehicle took a side street, vanishing from sight.

He drove for several more blocks before pulling over to the side of the road. He glanced at Alanna, his blood running cold as he realized members of the Blood Kings had likely been in the car behind them. Had taken shots at them.

And worse? They'd staked out his house, waiting for him to get home. How they'd known where he lived, he wasn't sure.

But that didn't change the grim realization that returning to his place had inadvertently put Alanna in harm's way for the second time that night.

CHAPTER THREE

"Who was in that car?" Alanna unclamped her fingers from her phone. Red-and-blue swirling lights brightened the night as cops raced toward them. She'd given the dispatcher directions on where they were the entire time Reed had been working to evade the gunmen.

Gunmen! She shivered.

"I don't know for sure, but I can hazard a guess." Reed gestured toward the two squads that flanked them. "Let's go. We'll need to give them our statements."

It was as if the nightmare within the emergency department had followed them here.

Was that it? She reached out to grab Reed's arm, preventing him from getting out of the vehicle. "This is gang related? Is that your theory?"

A flash of admiration lightened his blue eyes. "Yes. It's the only thing that makes sense."

She nodded, although the situation didn't make sense to her. Gang members focused on taking out rivals, not waging war against the police.

Except, Reed had killed Ivan Garcia. And two of his fellow gang members knew it.

Reed covered her hand with his. "Hey, it's going to be okay. Let's give our statements and go from there, okay?"

"Yes." She forced herself to release him, another chill snaking down her spine. She was accustomed to functioning in a crisis and using the one-step-at-a-time approach generally worked. But in this case, it wasn't a patient's life hanging in the balance.

It was Reed's life. And hers too.

Reed stepped forward, greeting the officers and describing what had transpired. The responding officers took note of the broken rear window. One climbed into the back seat, emerging a minute later with a bullet he'd taken from the center console.

"We'll get this processed," the officer said. "We can match it with the slugs found earlier at the shooting scene between Blood Kings and Latino Hombres."

"I'm sure they're still processing that crime scene." Reed raked his hand through his dark hair. "I don't like that they found my address. I know it sounds far-fetched, but I believe a member of the Blood Kings killed Wesley Durango too."

The officers exchanged a glance but didn't comment.

The name Wesley Durango didn't mean anything to her. She guessed that was the name of the murder victim Reed had mentioned earlier. The one that had made his squad a crime scene.

A murder and an attempted murder. Alanna's older siblings had gone through some difficult times over the past ten months, but she hadn't anticipated she'd be drawn into a similar situation.

Maybe she should have allowed Rhy to take her to the

homestead. Yet even as that thought flitted through her mind, she rejected it. She was deeply grateful she'd been with Reed. What if he'd have walked home alone? She had a bad feeling he would not have escaped unscathed.

She moved closer to Reed, shivering in her thin scrubs. He surprised her by placing his arm around her waist.

"If you don't have any more questions, we need to get out of here." Reed's tone was firm, as if he wasn't taking no as an answer.

"What about my car?" She waved a hand at the broken rear window. "Can I drive it, or does it have to be taken somewhere to be processed?"

"We don't need the vehicle," one of the officers assured her. "We have the bullet. There's no indication that the perps were close enough to leave any other evidence behind."

Reed nodded thoughtfully. "Okay, thanks. You have my contact information in case you have additional questions."

"Will do." The officers separated, each going to their respective squads.

"Your condo has underground parking, right?" Reed's voice was low, his gaze alert as he scanned the area.

"Yes." She frowned. "I don't want you staying at your place, Reed. It's too dangerous."

A rare smile creased his features. "I wasn't planning on it, but I don't want you to stay alone either. I realize you barely know me, but we need to drop off your car, then find a place to stay for the night."

Together? Her eyebrows rose as she considered his comment. "I don't think I'm in danger," she protested. "The car was near your house, Reed. Not mine."

"The shooter could have your license plate number. There's no way you can stay at your condo tonight." He gently ushered her to the car. "Let's drop this off in your parking garage, then decide our next steps."

She nodded, allowing him to slide into the driver's seat. As much as she didn't love the idea of going someplace else, she had to admit that was exactly what her cop brothers would have done.

Had in fact done more times in the past few months than she could count.

Reed took a winding route to her condo. The tag attached to her visor lifted the garage door to the underground parking area. The secure and underground parking had been one of the main reasons she'd purchased the condo. Living in the homestead, she'd often ended up parking outside, which meant cleaning snow and ice off her vehicle in the winter.

"I park in number seven." She waved toward the empty space.

Reed pulled in and shifted into park. "Is your condo number the same?"

"Yes." Understanding dawned. "Oh, you think one of the Blood Kings will figure out where I live by me parking my car here?"

"Yeah, I do." His blue gaze pierced hers. "Do not underestimate these guys. The Blood Kings and Latino Hombres are two gangs that have been running the streets of Milwaukee for years. Ever since a faction of them moved here from Chicago."

"But they're gang bangers, right? I mean, how would they have the resources needed to run my license plate number or find our respective addresses?" She scowled, pushing her car door open. "It doesn't make sense."

"I don't know." The hesitation in his tone made her think he had a theory on that too. A flash of annoyance hit hard. She had chosen nursing because she hadn't wanted to be a cop. Seeing her older siblings in action had only cemented that decision.

Between her headache and her sore incision, she abruptly slid from her damaged car. "I'm tired and hungry. I plan on staying in my condo tonight; you're welcome to sleep in the guest room."

"Alanna," he said on a sigh.

"Be serious, Reed. I highly doubt the Blood Kings will figure out my address, sneak into the underground parking garage, and then come up and break into my unit. They're not supermen. They're low-life thugs."

"Yeah, they are low-life thugs who killed a cop!"

His statement stopped her cold. "Wesley Durango was a cop?"

"Yes, a rookie." Reed moved closer, his expression serious in the dim light of the parking garage. "My partner. He was supposed to accompany Ivan Garcia to the hospital in cuffs. I blame myself for not following through to be sure he did as I directed. The shooting scene was chaotic. While I was tied up with two gang members, someone must have lured Wesley away, leaving Ivan Garcia in the ambulance alone. The EMTs should have questioned why a cop hadn't placed the victim in custody and ridden along but didn't."

"I see." She winced at what Rhy would say about that lapse. Yet she didn't blame Reed. Any of the cops on scene should have noticed the rookie was missing.

Chilling to realize the dead rookie was then placed in Reed's squad. As if the Blood Kings had known which vehicle they'd been in.

"Can we at least go up so I can shower and change?" She couldn't stand the thought of spending another minute in her bloodstained scrubs. "Please, Reed. You might want some different clothes to wear too. I have some shorts and a T-shirt that should fit you."

His brow arched. "Oh, you have a live-in boyfriend?"

"What? No!" Her cheeks grew warm. "The clothes belong to Aiden. My twin brother sometimes bunks in the guest room. Elly does too." As she said the words, she belatedly realized she didn't want any of her siblings stopping by the condo. Not until the gang members had been found and arrested.

"Okay, we'll spend a few minutes here so you can get cleaned up. But then we need to find a safe place. Somewhere no one would know to look for us."

She grudgingly nodded. Maybe he was right. When her older siblings had found themselves in danger, each of them had done whatever was necessary to keep the rest of the family safe from harm.

She might not be a cop, but she wouldn't let them down. Especially Elly. The youngest of the family had been sheltered by the rest of them. Her soft heart, evidenced by her tendency to bring stray animals and in one case a homeless guy home, didn't see strangers as threats. Quite the opposite. Elly tended to make friends with everyone.

Alanna led the way to the elevator, hitting the button for the second floor. The three-story building housed eighteen condos, six on each floor. She used her key to access her door, but Reed held her back from walking inside.

"I'll go first. Stay behind me."

She stifled a sigh as he entered her unit. He flipped on the lights, sweeping his gaze around the living and kitchen areas, before heading down the hall to the bedrooms. She closed and locked the door behind them when he was finished.

"How long will it take you to get ready?" He clearly

didn't want to stick around longer than necessary, but she refused to be rushed.

"You can find something to wear in the guest room. I'm taking a shower." She took her purse with her to the master bedroom, closing the door with a loud click. Then she leaned against it, her knees feeling weak.

She wasn't accustomed to this level of stress. To anticipating bad guys lurking around every corner. A bad day usually meant losing a patient despite doing everything in her power to save them.

Not being held hostage while a cop shoots and kills the patient holding you at knifepoint.

With resolute determination, she pushed herself away from the door to head into the bathroom. Enough wallowing in self-pity. She wasn't the one who'd been targeted by the Blood Kings. She hadn't used lethal force in her line of work and been subsequently placed on administrative leave.

She needed to do her part in keeping Reed safe. It was the least she could do for the man who'd saved her life.

REED DIDN'T WANT to stay in Alanna's condo for a minute longer than necessary. But when he heard the shower going, he knew they weren't hitting the road anytime soon.

Not that he had a car at his disposal. His was down at the police station where he'd left it prior to starting his shift. He had no plans to head down to get it either. After the incident at his place, driving a vehicle registered under his name was only asking for trouble.

Aiden's athletic pants and T-shirt fit well enough, but what he really needed was his backup weapon. Feeling downright naked without a gun, he seriously considered sneaking out of the condo to run the eight blocks to his place to grab it. It took all his willpower to wait.

He wouldn't leave Alanna alone and unprotected. Logically, he knew it would take time for the Blood Kings to find her address. They could stay for a short period of time before getting out of there.

It wasn't lost on him that he was the main reason she was in danger. He'd been the one to shoot Ivan "Ice" Garcia. And it was his house that had been staked out by the Blood Kings. As he paced her living room, he decided the best option would be to drop Alanna off with her brother Rhy. If he remembered correctly, Rhy lived in Brookland with his wife, Devon.

Not only would it be easier for him to stay under the radar without her, but she'd be safer too.

No question those bullets had been meant for him.

When Alanna finally emerged, she looked more beautiful than ever. He'd never seen her with her long blond hair waving around her shoulders. Or dressed in anything other than shapeless scrubs.

Her soft blue jeans and bright-yellow long-sleeved knit shirt hugged her sweet curves. He forced himself to look away lest he start drooling. *Get a grip*, he chided. Alanna was a victim, not a potential date. Maybe he'd considered asking her out, but not now. Not after everything that had happened. Clearing his throat, he managed to keep his tone light. "Great. I'm glad you're ready."

"I'm not leaving until we eat something." She gave him a steely look as she opened the fridge. "Luckily, I have leftover chili, so it won't take too long. I'm not sure when you last ate, but you're welcome to join me."

He swallowed a groan and forced a smile. The clock on

the stove indicated the hour was close to nine fifteen at night, but he decided sharing a quick meal wouldn't hurt. "Sure. Chili sounds good." He hadn't eaten in hours, and as she nuked the leftovers, the spicy scent made his mouth water.

"Have a seat." She shot him an amused glance over her shoulder. "Too bad I took the leftover corn bread to work today. Those scavengers ate every last bite."

"You made corn bread?" He wished she hadn't mentioned it because now he was drooling for real. "I'm impressed."

"I don't mind cooking." She shrugged and opened the microwave to stir the chili. "I don't always bother, though, since I live alone."

He watched her as she brought the bowl of chili to the table. "You don't have a boyfriend?"

"Not anymore." She didn't elaborate, although he was curious as to what happened. She spooned the leftover chili into two bowls, giving him the larger one. Then she surprised him by clasping her hands together and bowing her head. "Dear Lord Jesus, we thank You for this food we are about to eat. We ask that You keep Reed safe in Your care and that the investigation into his shooting is deemed appropriate. Amen."

"Amen." He sat for a moment before reaching for his spoon. "No one has ever prayed for me before."

She looked surprised. "I've prayed for you often over the past several months."

"Really?" Her admission was humbling. "Why?"

She blushed. "Because you and all police officers on the job, like my brothers and sister, need God's protection. You place yourself in harm's way to keep the rest of us safe. The better question is why wouldn't I pray for you? For all officers and first responders putting themselves in the line of fire."

"That's very sweet." A few bad apples in the cop ranks had ruined the overall appreciation of police first responders for the rest of them. He was secretly amazed that she'd cared enough to include him in her prayers.

"Don't keep me in suspense," she joked as he tried the chili. "Do you love it or hate it?"

"It's very good." He grinned, feeling lighthearted despite the danger lurking nearby. "I'm impressed, Ms. Finnegan."

She rolled her eyes. "Does that mean you thought I was useless in the kitchen?"

"Never." Her kitchen skills or lack thereof had never entered his mind. He'd been drawn to her because of her beauty and her caring attitude toward her patients. Even those in police custody had been treated with kindness and respect.

That wasn't always the case. He'd heard some of the staff spouting off in derogatory terms about the trauma patients they cared for. Truthfully, he could understand how staff may become irritated at taking care of gunshot wounds and knife injuries. Like cops, medical staff could become jaded.

But not Alanna. No matter how badly the patients treated her, she always maintained a professional attitude.

And he hoped this recent incident with Garcia wouldn't change that for her.

"How long have you worked in the ED?"

"Five years. Aiden and I just turned twenty-eight last month." She took a spoonful of chili, then added, "I had to work the general medical-surgical unit for a year before I could transfer to the emergency department. Those nurses work hard; they're stuck with the same patient for the entire shift and sometimes for days in a row." She wrinkled her nose. "I prefer the emergency department where patients come and go throughout the shift."

"Even after tonight?" As soon as the question left his mouth, he wanted it back.

A shadow darkened her brown eyes. "Yes, even after tonight. Although I'll take a hard pass on being held hostage again."

"I'm sorry." He could have kicked himself for being so dense. He reached for her hand. "I shouldn't have reminded you."

"It's okay." Her smile didn't reach her eyes. "But I have a new appreciation for what you face each day, Reed. It must be difficult to remain on high alert at all times."

"You get used to it." That wasn't entirely true, but he didn't want her to worry.

She tipped her head to the side as if sensing he wasn't being honest. Then she asked, "What's the plan anyway? Do you have an idea on where we can go?"

He ate another bite of chili before answering. "I was thinking you should call one of your brothers, either Rhy or Tarin, to stay with them for a few days. I'd rather not expose you to any more danger."

"No thank you." Her tone was polite, but she narrowed her eyes.

"Be reasonable." He tried not to show his impatience. "Your safety is important. I know Rhy and Tarin would agree with me."

"First of all, you said yourself the gunman might be able to get my address from my license plate." She pointed her spoon at him. "Secondly, Rhy's wife, Devon, is pregnant with their first child. She's due the end of next month. And

I have reason to believe Tarin's wife, Joy, may be pregnant too, although they haven't made that announcement."

The pregnancy news took him by surprise. "How do you know Tarin's wife is pregnant?"

"Because she stopped drinking coffee. No sane person does that unless they have to avoid caffeine for some important reason."

He couldn't help but smile. "Not everyone likes coffee."

"Joy does, and she's refused any the last few times we had family gatherings together." She shook her head. "I'm not going to stay with either of them. Or anyone else in my family. That would only bring the danger to their doorstep. Sorry, Reed. You're stuck with me."

There was no one he'd rather be stuck with, but he managed to keep that thought to himself. "Okay, then I need one favor from you."

She eyed him suspiciously. "What kind of favor?"

"I need to head back to my place to get my backup gun. I'd like you to wait here for me."

She frowned. "You said earlier that it's better if we stick together."

"Not this time." Especially not since his house had been staked out earlier. "I did say that, yes. And I don't want to leave you here. But I need you to do this for me. It won't take me long to get into my place to get my weapon. I need to be armed in order to keep you safe."

"Okay." Her grudging agreement had him letting his breath out in a soundless sigh. It wasn't optimal for her to stay here, but he hoped she'd be safe enough for the ten minutes it would take him to get his piece.

"Thank you." He glanced around her tidy condo. "Do you have a weapon here?"

"Why would I?" She sounded annoyed. "Just because

most of my brothers and my sister Kyleigh carry guns doesn't mean we all do."

"You have knives, right?" He arched a brow. "That's a weapon."

"I don't think I could bring myself to use it."

"Alanna." He held her gaze. "You know that's not true. If there had been a weapon nearby earlier this evening, I have no doubt you'd have used it against Ivan Garcia."

She didn't answer, but the resigned expression in her eyes indicated she knew he was right. He let it go, quickly finishing his meal. Leaving even for a short time didn't sit well, but he absolutely needed his backup piece.

"Do me a favor and lock yourself in the bathroom with a knife until I return."

"What?" She gaped at him. "That's ridiculous."

Clenching his jaw, he stared back. "It's not. Better to be prepared."

"I'll be fine." She stood and carried her empty chili bowl to the sink. "Just go, Reed. I'm sure you'll be back by the time I finish washing dishes."

He finished his meal, then joined her. "Seriously, Alanna. I need you to be prepared for the worst. And I need your phone number, so I can text you when I'm back. I don't want you to open the front door for anyone, understand?"

"I'm not an idiot." She dried her hands and pulled out her phone. He typed in her number as she rattled it off. Then he called her so she'd have his number as well.

Not exactly the way he'd wanted to get her number, but there was nothing he could do about that. He gathered his uniform together and then left the condo.

A sense of urgency plagued him as he took the stairs down to the main entryway. He peered through the glass door, then slid out and jogged around the corner to the back of the building.

He ran seven blocks without breaking a sweat. Then he slowed and cut through the yards of the houses along the last block so that he could approach his place from the rear, staying away from the well-lit road outside his home.

Once inside, he stood for a moment, allowing his eyes to adjust to the darkness. He didn't turn on any lights, unwilling to alert anyone who may still be watching. Moving quickly and silently, he made his way to the bedroom and opened the lockbox holding his backup weapon. He stripped off the borrowed clothes in favor of his own things. He changed his shoes, too, ditching the clunky black shoes all cops were required to wear. Then he added his belt holster and secured his weapon. He stuffed additional ammo into the pocket of his black leather jacket, along with some plastic flex cuffs on the off chance he might need them.

After spending less than three minutes inside, Reed left via the back door as silently as he'd come. He broke into a jog to get back to Alanna's condo, telling himself she was fine despite the niggling feeling at the back of his neck.

He slowed his pace two blocks from the condo, ducking behind a tree when headlights pierced the darkness. He didn't believe the vehicle belonged to the Blood Kings; earlier they'd driven without lights.

Reassured once the vehicle passed by, he resumed his trek to the condo. A shadow of movement caught his eye, and he paused near a tree, searching the darkness.

Was he letting his imagination run away with him? Reed told himself to stop being paranoid. He was about to step away from the tree when he saw two men dressed in hoodies cross the street just twenty yards from him.

The niggle of warning coalesced into full-blown alarm. He quickly texted Alanna a warning, then followed the two suspects. Within seconds, they split up, each going around the other side of the condo building.

He dialed 911, even though he knew that by the time the police arrived, it would be too late.

CHAPTER FOUR

Reed's text flashed on her screen. *Two men in hoodies outside your building. Take cover.*

Remembering how she'd been held hostage, Alanna's heart jumped in her throat. She shut off all the lights, then ducked into the bathroom. She locked the door, then backed away, pressing her hands against her chest. Should she get in the shower? No, if these guys started shooting, the shower curtain wouldn't protect her.

She'd forgotten the knife! Too late now, she wasn't going back out to the kitchen to get it. Besides, a knife only worked if the bad guys got close enough for her to use it. Struggling to draw a deep breath, she glanced around the bathroom.

The heavy top of the toilet tank caught her attention. Like the knife, it wouldn't help unless the bad guys came inside. But she picked it up anyway, then positioned herself behind the door on the side where the hinges were located. If one of them kicked the door open, she might be able to clobber him in the head before he saw her.

Two men with hoodies. If they both managed to get all

the way inside her condo, she had little hope of holding off two men. Two likely armed men.

Swallowing hard, she sent up a silent prayer. *Lord Jesus, please keep me and Reed safe in Your care!*

Her parents had raised them with faith, and when Rhy and Tarin had taken over after their death, their faith had held them together as a family. She often leaned on prayer, especially working in the emergency department.

But she'd never been in the center of danger the way she'd been today. First at work and again now.

The silence was deafening. She strained to listen but could only hear the thundering beat of her heart. Drawing in a long, slow deep breath, she attempted to calm herself. Panic wouldn't help. In the ED, she was known to be cool and calm during emergency situations. Granted, those situations weren't dangerous, but they were often life or death.

She could do this!

The silence in her condo was bad, but hearing nothing from Reed was worse. Was he trying to take out the two men, himself? She shivered. He was well trained and armed, but it was still two against one.

Her arms began to ache, forcing her to lower the toilet tank top to the floor. *Time to renew my gym membership,* she thought grimly. *Hauling patients around obviously isn't good enough. I've turned into a weakling. A marshmallow weakling.*

A thudding sound had her abruptly straightening. What was that? Had someone gotten inside?

A surge of adrenaline had her lifting the heavy toilet tank top above her head again. For several long seconds, she didn't hear anything more. Her imagination? Or maybe the sound was simply her neighbor's door closing.

Then the bathroom door handle jiggled.

Biting down on her lip to keep from screaming, she stood stock-still waiting for the hoodie guy to kick the flimsy door in.

Or worse, shoot through it.

Another loud thud reached her ears. Was the second hoodie guy in the house too?

Her arms trembled with the exertion of holding the toilet tank cover over her head. She held her breath, waiting for the bathroom to be breached.

A shout rang out, followed by more loud thuds. After what seemed like eons, she heard her name.

"Alanna? It's Reed. Are you okay?"

The voice sounded like Reed's, but she found herself hesitating in case this was a trick. But she couldn't hold up the toilet tank cover any longer, so she lowered it to the floor and called, "Reed? Is it really you?"

"Yes. Hang on." A second later, her phone vibrated in her pocket. Propping the toilet seat cover against the wall, she glanced at the screen to read his text. *You're safe. I have one guy in cuffs. The other got away.*

Reed caught one of them? She quickly replaced the tank cover, then gingerly opened the bathroom door. Peeking out, she could see two dark shapes in her living area. One was standing, the other was lying stretched out on the floor with his arms behind his back. "Reed?"

"Yeah, I'm here. Go pack a bag." The words were not a suggestion. "We're getting out of here as soon as the cops arrive to take this guy into custody."

"I didn't do nothin'," the hoodie guy muttered.

"Breaking and entering for starters," Reed said calmly. He flicked on a light, causing her to blink to adjust to the brightness. "And I bet that gun I took off you isn't legal either."

Gun? A wave of dizziness hit hard. This man had come very close to getting to her in the bathroom. If Reed hadn't noticed him and warned her . . .

She turned away, bracing herself with a hand on the wall, her knees shaky. Abruptly straightening, she forced herself to move to the bedroom. She'd already changed clothes, but now she grabbed the gym bag she hadn't used in over four months and stuffed a change of clothes in beside her small travel case of toiletries.

The all-too familiar sound of police sirens filled the night. As she joined Reed in the living area, she could see red-and-blue flashing lights through her window.

Her knees threatened to give out again, so she set her duffel on the small kitchen table and leaned against it. She hated feeling weak and helpless. Yet seeing the cuffed man on her living room floor was surreal. None of this made any sense, especially if the guy Reed had cuffed was a member of the Blood Kings.

Gangs didn't stalk and kill nurses. The logic of this attack escaped her.

Of course, this guy had probably come for Reed. He must have gotten her address from her license plate. Yet even that seemed a stretch. Everyday gang members didn't have those kinds of resources.

"Alanna?" Reed's low voice caught her attention. She lifted her head to look at him. "You'll want to let the police in."

"Sure." She pushed herself away from the table and went over to the intercom system that was buzzing from below. She pressed the button to unlock the door. "How did this guy get past the security?"

"I think he must have gotten into the parking garage."

Reed's grim gaze met hers. "We should have left right away."

He was right, and it was her fault they hadn't. "We're safe now. And you having one of them in custody should help, right? Maybe the police will convince him to talk."

"Lawyer," the bound guy said in a loud voice.

"Maybe," Reed agreed, ignoring the guy he'd cuffed. He stared at her for a long moment, then glanced toward the door of her condo. It hung ajar, making her realize the lock must have been broken. Or breached in some way.

How? She'd had the deadbolt on and hadn't heard anything loud enough to indicate the door had been kicked in.

Two uniformed police officers came into her condo. "Reed Carmichael?"

"That's me." Reed gestured to the man on the floor. "This man unlawfully entered the premises with the intent to harm the condo owner, Alanna Finnegan."

"Finnegan?" The officer closest to her raised a brow. "Related to Rhy and Tarin?"

"My brothers." She noted his name tag identified him as Officer Cohen. "I don't understand how this man got inside my condo."

"Lock picks," Reed held up several slim-looking tools. "I took these off him when I searched for weapons. He had a thirty-eight special too."

Having a gun wasn't unusual for a gang banger, but lock picks? She stared at the cuffed man who hadn't uttered a word since the cops arrived.

The two officers crossed over to haul the perp to his feet. This guy had a teardrop tattoo near his eye, but it wasn't red in color, it was only drawn on his face. She knew that in the gang world, an empty teardrop indicated he'd injured someone but hadn't killed them.

Small consolation.

It took well over an hour for her and Reed to provide their statements to the responding officer. Once they began, they had to go back and fill them in on the events that had unfolded in the ED and the shooting that had taken place outside Reed's house.

The time was going on eleven o'clock by the time they'd finished. She reached for her duffel, but Reed took it from her fingers. "Let's go downstairs and grab a rideshare."

"Okay." She was too exhausted to argue. "But we'll need a car at some point."

"I know. We'll worry about that tomorrow." Reed rested his hand in the small of her back as they took the stairs down to the first floor. Outside, she could see the officers in their respective squads, the perp sitting in the back seat behind the cage in Cohen's vehicle.

It reminded her of Reed's dead partner who'd been placed in their squad. It hit her hard that the man sitting there had intended to add to the body count by killing her and Reed too.

For what? Revenge? It was the only explanation she could come up with.

Reed glanced up from his phone, catching her gaze. The harsh planes of his face softened. "You're going to be okay, Alanna."

"I know." She shivered, remembering those tense moments in the bathroom. She'd never wanted to carry a gun, but she was glad Reed was armed. Her brothers had taken her to the shooting range, a requirement their father had initiated. Most of her siblings owned guns. Colin didn't carry, and neither did Elly.

It was tempting to call Rhy to ask for a weapon, but she refrained. Her oldest brother would want to hear the entire story and would try to insist she come to the homestead, despite Devon's pregnancy.

Better to keep him out of this for a while.

A white SUV pulled to the curb. Reed stepped forward to speak through the passenger-side window with the driver. Then he opened the back door and gestured for her to climb in.

"You're heading to the Timberland Falls Suites?" the driver asked.

"That's correct." Reed clipped his seatbelt, then reached for her hand.

"Got it." The driver had already put the information into the phone mounted on his dash. She gratefully clung to Reed's hand as the rideshare driver navigated the streets. Timberland Falls wasn't far, roughly fourteen miles from her condo. Hopefully, it was enough of a distance that the Blood Kings wouldn't find them.

She'd never known any gang members to operate outside of the Milwaukee neighborhoods they ruled. In some ways, it wasn't smart of them to venture to the suburban areas where men with teardrop tattoos stood out like sore thumbs.

Then again, crime happened everywhere.

Traffic was light at this hour, and they made it to the Timberland Falls hotel in less than fifteen minutes. Reed thanked the driver, slung her duffel over his shoulder, then escorted her inside. Without asking her opinion, he requested a two-bedroom suite on the first floor. She knew he'd requested that specifically for a quick getaway.

It must be exhausting to constantly plan an escape route.

"I can help pay." She reached for the zipper on the duffel to retrieve her purse.

"No need. I've got it." He handed over his credit card, then waited for the clerk to hand over their room keys.

Their room wasn't too far from the lobby. Reed unlocked the door, then held it open for her. The accommodations were nice; there was a small central living space with two bedrooms located on each side.

"Well." She stood in the center of the room for a moment. "I guess this is home sweet home for the foreseeable future."

"Yeah." Reed set her duffel on the sofa. His solemn gaze met hers. "I'm sorry. I never should have left you in the condo alone."

She could tell he was beating himself up over it. "I'm fine. And you caught one of the bad guys, which is a big deal. I'm sure once he sits in jail for a while, he'll talk in exchange of leniency."

"I hope so." His blue eyes darkened. "I hate knowing you're in danger because of me."

"It's okay." She stepped closer, putting her hand on his arm. "I'm glad we're together."

"Me too." His low voice was husky with emotion. His gaze dropped to her mouth, then quickly darted away. Reed abruptly stepped back. "Ah, we need to get some sleep."

Without waiting for her to respond, he picked up her duffel and carried it into one of the bedrooms. Then he emerged and crossed over to the second bedroom.

"Good night." He barely glanced at her as he shut the door behind him.

She stared at his closed door for a moment, then turned to head into her room. Sleep wouldn't come easily, but her body craved rest.

Almost as much as she'd craved Reed's kiss.

***

THAT WAS A CLOSE ONE. Not just one of the hoodie perps getting inside Alanna's condo, but the kiss he'd narrowly avoided.

Hadn't he screwed up enough? Kissing Alanna was way out of line. His actions had dragged her into this mess. The two gang members had staked out his house and had only gone to Alanna's condo because they'd expected to find him there.

He sank down onto the edge of the bed, propping his elbows on his knees and holding his head in his hands. If Rhy or Tarin knew what he'd done, they'd beat him to a pulp.

Well, maybe they wouldn't resort to physical violence, but they'd tear a strip off his back for putting their baby sister in harm's way. If he hadn't managed to scare off the first hoodie guy in time to get up into the condo to prevent the second one from getting to Alanna, he'd be facing the Finnegan wrath right now.

And he'd deserve it.

The chili they'd eaten churned in his belly. They shouldn't have lingered to eat. He should have taken her with him to his place.

Enough. He stood and paced the room. Time to pull himself together. He needed to keep his head in the deadly game these Blood Kings seemed intent on playing. Which meant holding Alanna at a professional distance. They were safe for now, but he needed a better plan come morning.

What that entailed, he had no clue.

Images from the evening flashed through his mind.

Alanna being held at knifepoint, dragged across the room. His rookie partner's dead body falling out of their squad. The gunfire from the car without lights. And finding Alanna's condo door open with a gang member moving silently inside.

He wasn't on duty but considered calling one of his cop buddies for help. He was fairly certain Geoff Watkins was home from his shift by now; he'd come to the initial scene of the shooting among several others. He'd also likely heard the news of Reed being placed on administrative leave.

Then again, why bother him now? He'd call Geoff in the morning before his friend's second shift tour started. There was nothing Geoff could do for him tonight.

Reed headed into the bathroom, hoping a shower would clear his head. Afterward, he felt better but still too keyed up to sleep.

His phone on the bedside table vibrated. He snatched it up, frowning at the unknown number.

After a moment's hesitation, he answered it. "Yeah?"

"Carmichael, what in the world is going on?"

It took him a minute to realize the caller was one of Alanna's brothers. "Who is this? And how did you get my personal cell number?"

"This is Rhy, and I have connections. Now tell me what happened? Why am I hearing about a break-in at my sister's condo through the cop grapevine?"

He swung up to sit on the side of the bed. "For one thing, I don't have your number. I take it Alanna didn't call you?"

"No, and she should have. So should you." Rhy sounded upset, and Reed couldn't blame the guy. He'd be mad too if his sister was in danger.

"I'm sorry, it's my fault." Reed dragged his hands over

his hair. "After the gunfire outside my house, I should have gotten Alanna far away."

"Gunfire? What gunfire?" Rhy's voice rose in volume, making him wince.

Apparently, the grapevine hadn't included that part of the story. "My house is only eight blocks from Alanna's condo. We swung by there, and a car drove up without headlights. Someone took a few shots at us, breaking the rear window of Alanna's car."

"Wait a minute. Why were you and Alanna together at your place?" Rhy's tone reeked of suspicion. "Are you taking advantage of my baby sister, Carmichael?"

"No, I'm not." Although he had nearly kissed her. Something he had no plan of revealing to Alanna's oldest brother. "I walked her to her car after work. I didn't have my vehicle there, so she offered me a ride home. I declined, but she seemed pretty shaken up, so I offered to drive her car to her condo, intending to walk to my house from there since I only live eight blocks away. She didn't believe me and insisted I show her where I live. Something I wouldn't have done if I'd have known two gang bangers were waiting."

There was a long silence as Rhy digested his statement. "How would gang bangers know where you live?"

"I don't know. To be honest, none of this makes sense." He was glad Rhy's questions had turned to the case rather than his younger sister. "And even more confounding is that they must have gotten Alanna's license plate number because they showed up at her condo. I know we weren't followed there because we called 911 and had the police come to us several blocks away from her place and mine."

"You're right, that doesn't make sense. Milwaukee gangs are all about drug and firearm dealing along with prostitution. They don't have access to the general public's personal information."

"I hear what you're saying, but I'm telling you, they found her there," Reed repeated. "I managed to grab one of them, so maybe the police will convince him to talk. Although he had nothing to say while I was there."

"I don't like this," Rhy muttered.

Reed didn't much like it either. And since Rhy was a cop, he decided to tell him the entire story. "There's one more thing you should know. My partner, a rookie cop by the name of Wesley Durango, was supposed to accompany Ivan 'Ice' Garcia to the hospital."

"Why didn't he?" Rhy asked.

"I'm not sure what happened, I was taking two of the Latino Hombres into custody myself. Knowing Wes was a rookie was the main reason I rushed to the hospital to check on Garcia when I finished at the scene. That's when I saw he had Alanna hostage. After shooting him, I went out to my squad and found Wesley Durango's dead body, a bullet hole in the center of his forehead."

"You're saying the Blood Kings killed a cop?" Rhy's tone sounded incredulous.

"Someone at the scene of the shooting did, and there were several gang members who took off when we arrived. Members of both the Latino Hombres and the Blood Kings."

Rhy let out a low whistle. "Pretty bold to execute a cop."

"Tell me about it." Reed rubbed the back of his neck. "I guess they're coming after me for revenge, but even that is unusual. Gangs generally stay away from shooting and killing cops."

"There's nothing usual about this case." Rhy sighed

loudly. "As far as I know, using Alanna as a hostage to escape being arrested has never happened before."

"Not to my knowledge," Reed agreed.

"Where are you and Alanna now?"

He hesitated, bracing himself for another outburst. "We're in a two-bedroom suite outside of Milwaukee, in Timberland Falls. The biggest problem right now is that we don't have a set of wheels. We had to use a rideshare to get out of the city."

"I can help with that," Rhy said. "Since you're settled someplace safe, I'll arrange for you to have a car by morning."

"Okay, thanks." Reed figured Rhy was going out of his way to help out of concern for his sister, and that was fine with him. He wanted Alanna safe too. "Let's connect tomorrow morning."

"Fine." There was a brief pause before Rhy added, "You better watch yourself, Carmichael. I expect my sister treated with respect, understand?"

"Yes, sir." Rhy held the rank of captain, and Reed had no doubt that Rhy would make it his mission to ruin his career if anything bad happened to Alanna.

Not that he had much of a career now. Thanks to the video footage outside the hospital's ED entrance, he wasn't a suspect in Wesley Durango's murder, but his partner had been snatched from the scene of the shooting without any of the responding officers noticing.

Far from stellar police work, he thought with a wince. Shooting a suspect was bad enough, but the entire fiasco would be investigated by the internal affairs department along with the upper brass.

He crawled back into bed, determined to get some

sleep. Just knowing he'd have Rhy's support helped him relax.

Nice to know he wasn't alone in this.

Reed must have fallen asleep because the next thing he knew, his phone was buzzing again. With a low groan, he picked it up, squinting at the screen.

Who was calling at five thirty in the morning? Not Rhy's number, but one that looked familiar. Someone within his precinct. Not that any of the bigwigs showed up at work this early in the morning.

He cautiously answered. "Yeah?"

"Carmichael? It's Simmons. Chuck Simmons."

He recognized one of the newer night-shift officers. "What's up? You know I'm on administrative leave, right?" He figured the guy was calling to swap shifts or something.

"Yeah, I know. I'm calling you from the bathroom." Okay, that was an image he hadn't needed. "I wanted to let you know because I don't know if anyone else will."

Maybe he was still sleep deprived because he didn't understand what Chuck was talking about. "Tell me what?"

"There's a price on your head." Chuck's voice dropped to a whisper. "We heard from a source on the street that the Blood Kings have put the word out that anyone who kills you will get five grand."

A chill snaked down his spine. "That seems on the cheap side to shoot a cop."

"Don't joke," Simmons said in a grim tone. "This is serious stuff. The source claims every member in the Blood Kings gang is looking for you."

Simmons was right, the situation wasn't funny. "I appreciate the heads-up."

"You need to get out of town, Reed. Stay far away until things have settled down."

"I'll do that." Technically, he was out of town. "Thanks again for calling."

"You didn't hear it from me. Watch your back." With that, Simmons disconnected the call.

Reed set his phone down, his fellow officer's words sinking deep. Killing Ivan Garcia was coming back to bite him in the butt. And while he normally wouldn't care about a bunch of gang bangers with a grudge against him, these guys had already proven their keen determination to make him pay.

With his life.

CHAPTER FIVE

Alanna woke with a start, her heart thumping as the remnants of her nightmare faded. She lifted a hand to her incision, shivering as she reassured herself the nightmare wasn't real. In her dream, Ivan Garcia had slit her throat, then somehow had a gun in hand and started shooting everyone in sight. The medical staff, the security guards.

Even Reed.

Swallowing hard, she pushed her hair from her damp skin. Glancing at her phone, she noted the time to be five minutes before six in the morning. She'd always preferred day shifts in the ED; her natural sleep cycle was to wake up early.

Despite the horrifying dream, she'd slept better than expected. Her room had its own bathroom, so she rummaged in her duffel to find the clear dressings Dana had given her. After carefully applying one over her tender incision, she ducked into the shower.

Feeling refreshed afterward, Alanna pulled on the extra set of clean clothes she'd brought along. The enticing scent of coffee indicated Reed was already up and about. She opened her door and stepped into the living area.

"Good morning." She couldn't help feeling a bit awkward at sharing personal space with a man she'd only known through work.

"Good morning." His smile didn't quite reach his eyes. "The coffee is just about ready. I figured we'd call room service for breakfast too."

"Sounds good." She searched his gaze for a moment, sensing he was hiding something. "What's up? Did you hear something about the gang member you took into custody last night?"

He nodded as he filled a mug with coffee, then handed it to her. "I have news to share, but we should order breakfast first."

The news must not be good. She added cream and sugar to her coffee, then took the in-room dining menu from him. "I'll have two eggs over easy with toast and bacon."

"Okay. Give me a minute to place the order." He phoned in their breakfast request, his choice mirroring hers, then brought his coffee to the sofa. She scooted over to give him room. His nearness had her remembering their almost kiss.

She shook off the thought to focus on the reason they were stuck there in the first place. "Okay, spill it. Why do I get the feeling you have bad news?"

"Not all bad. I spoke to your brother Rhy last night."

She groaned. "I should have called him when we got here. What happened? Did he interrogate you over the condo incident?"

"He did." A hint of a smile tugged at the corner of Reed's mouth. "I have to say, it could have been worse. He was fairly decent considering your life is in danger."

"He's overprotective, especially of me and Elly. The youngest," she clarified.

"You mentioned eight siblings. Remind me again who they are and what they do?"

Maybe it was a stall tactic, but she obliged, ticking them off on her fingers. "Rhy is the oldest and is the captain of the tactical unit. He's married to Devon who is pregnant with their first child due mid-November. Tarin is second in line; he's an MPD detective and married to Joy. Like I mentioned, I believe she might be pregnant too. Kyleigh works as a sheriff's deputy for Milwaukee County. She's married to ADA Bax Scala. Brady is fourth oldest; he's with the FBI and is married to Grace. They have a six-year-old son named Caleb. Quinn is the fifth in line; he's with the Coast Guard and is married to Sami, who is an MPD cop too."

"I know Sami," Reed said with a nod. "She's great."

"She is; we love her." Alanna went back to listing her siblings. "Colin is a firefighter and recently married Faye; she's an ED doc." Thinking of Faye made Alanna glad her sister-in-law wasn't working the day she'd been taken hostage. "My twin brother Aiden is three minutes older than me; he's with the National Guard. Then after me there's Elly. We call her the oops baby. She's the youngest and has been working as an EMT."

"That's quite a lineup." He smiled, for real this time. "I'm impressed so many of your family members are cops."

"Our dad was a cop, and my mom was a nurse. They met in the ED." Her cheeks went pink as she unwittingly drew a parallel between her parents and the way she'd met Reed. She averted her gaze, hoping he didn't notice. "They emphasized that serving others is the most important thing we could do. That mindset was reinforced at church. We all took their example to heart; although honestly, we're a bit concerned about Elly. It's taken her a while to find her niche, and we're not convinced the EMT route is for her."

Reed arched a brow. "But she's working as an EMT now, right?"

"Yes." Alanna shrugged. "I can't really explain it, but I don't get the sense she loves going to work."

"I'm sure there are days you don't like going to work."

"Yeah, but it's something else. More like she's experiencing trepidation." She sipped her coffee. "She'll figure it out, and we'll support her no matter what she decides to do."

"Your family sounds amazing." Reed stared down at his coffee for a long moment. "I have an older brother in the army. We don't get to see each other very often. Our parents split up well over ten years ago now, so we don't have many happy family gatherings."

"I'm sorry to hear that." She couldn't help reaching out to touch his arm. "It's hard for me to imagine since I grew up in a household full of love and support. And chaos," she added with a smile. "Lots of chaos."

Reed turned to face her. "I better understand Rhy's concern last night. We need to keep your brother in the loop moving forward. I'm going to touch base with him after breakfast. He's going to help us get access to a car."

The news didn't surprise her. When her older siblings had been in danger before, the rest of the family had rallied around, swapping vehicles often to help each other hide under the radar. Aiden was the most cost conscious of the group and had secretly bemoaned his precious truck being damaged by a fire back in August while he'd supported Colin and Faye. "Rhy is good at pitching in to help out."

"I can tell." Reed's expression turned serious. "The

second call I received was from a fellow officer in my district. Apparently, the Blood Kings have offered a five-grand reward to anyone who kills me."

"What?" She stared at him in horror. "That's terrible."

"Yeah, it's not good." He tried to smile, but she could tell he was concerned. "I think it's best if you head back to the homestead with your brother. I'll go off-grid until the investigation into my shooting Garcia is completed."

"No, Reed. I don't want to put Devon in danger." She set her coffee down and turned on the sofa to face him. "What are the police doing about this threat? Who's taking the lead on bringing the Blood Kings gang down?"

"I don't know." Reed slowly shook his head. "I didn't hear about the bounty through official channels. The cop who called me heard the info from a source on the street."

"The police department must be doing something about this." The idea that every gang member or even non-gang members who wanted extra cash would be coming after Reed filled her with fear and dread. No way could she let him take off on his own. "Your life is in danger, Reed. And really, every cop on the force's life is on the line too. Some idiot might mistake another cop for you and shoot to kill."

"I've been thinking about that," Reed admitted. "I'm hoping to get in touch with my lieutenant. He should be in after seven thirty. He may know more about what strategies are being used to combat this attack."

She wasn't satisfied and continued pacing the suite. Knowing Reed was the main target was bad enough, but what if Sami, Rhy, Tarin, or any of the other officers she knew got caught in the crossfire? She highly doubted any gang member would give a rip if they killed the wrong cop.

More likely, they'd use it as a badge of honor. Another teardrop tattoo.

She abruptly spun to face him. "Does Rhy know about this?"

"Not yet." Reed stood and came to stand beside her. "I'll tell him this morning, but you seriously need to stay away from me. I'm the one with a target on my back. I don't want you to get hurt."

"They came to my condo, remember? I'm already involved." She wasn't a cop, so she knew her skills were rather useless. But she would not leave Reed alone. "We need to stick together. If someone is desperate enough for the cash, they might track me down to the homestead. I won't put my family at risk, Reed. No matter what."

They stared at each other, both frustrated and upset. A knock at the door broke the tension. "Room service."

Reed sighed and stepped back. "I'll get it."

While he tipped the server and carried the tray of food to the table, she texted her brother Rhy. *Blood Kings put a price of 5K on Reed's head.*

Instantly, three little dots indicated her brother was responding. *Not good. Call me.*

She turned to walk into her room, lifting the phone to her ear as Rhy answered. "Are you sure about this?" her brother demanded.

"Reed heard about it from a fellow cop in his district." She felt Reed coming up behind her, so she turned to face him. No sense in pretending she wasn't talking to her brother. "We need to plan our next move. And I'm worried about all of you too. Every cop is in danger with this bounty."

"Of course we are." Rhy sounded disgusted. "Aiden is on his way back to Milwaukee. He wants to be involved."

"I told you not to tell Aiden. I knew he'd cut his trip short." She was annoyed Rhy hadn't listened to her.

"Calm down, sis. It wasn't my idea, he called me as if sensing you were in trouble." There was a pause before Rhy added, "I'll be in touch in an hour. I need time to gather more intel and for Aiden to get here. We'll meet you at the hotel before you check out, okay? Where are you staying?"

"At the Timberland Falls Suites. But know this, I'm sticking with Reed until this is over."

"Stubborn," Rhy muttered. "We'll discuss that more later."

"Later, then." She disconnected from the call. "Rhy and Aiden will be swinging by in a few hours. In the meantime, Rhy is going to find out more about what the police are doing."

"That would be helpful." Reed held her gaze. "I know Rhy isn't going to let you stay with me, and that's fine. I totally understand. The sooner you go along with the plan, the faster we can move on."

She resisted the urge to throw her phone at him, feeling certain it would shatter against his thick skull. Striving to remain calm, she brushed past him toward the tray of food. "I'm hungry. Let's eat."

He followed her to the small table. She took a moment to refill their coffee cups, then sat across from him.

Bowing her head, she let out a breath. Anger was never useful. She sought patience instead. "Dear Lord, we thank You for this food we are about to eat. We ask that You continue to guide us on Your path while providing us the wisdom we need to fight the evil men coming after us. Amen."

"Amen," Reed echoed. "But the evil men are after me, Alanna. Not you."

"Both of us." She lightly touched the skin at her neck. The incision still hurt if she turned her head too quickly, but the stitches weren't red or inflamed from infection. She was fortunate the injury wasn't worse.

His mouth tightened as he eyed the line of sutures. They ate in silence for several minutes. She understood his concern for her safety; she had the same worry for his. But even he should be able to figure out they were better off staying together.

Finally, she said, "Leaving me alone at the condo didn't work out so well. If you care about me and my family at all, you'll allow me to stay close."

He closed his eyes, then lifted his tortured gaze. "Don't you understand? It's because I care about you that I want you safely away from me."

His words eased the remnants of her anger. "Please know the feeling is mutual. And it's because I care that we need to stick together."

"I never met anyone as stubborn as you," he muttered, stabbing an egg with his fork.

"Back at you." She didn't care if he was annoyed. The only thing that mattered to her was making sure the Blood Kings didn't succeed in their mission.

Deep down, she knew God had brought them together for a reason. And no matter what Rhy or Aiden said, she was going to stay with Reed until the danger was over.

REED COULDN'T DECIDE whether he wanted to throttle Alanna or kiss her. She was the most endearing and frustrating woman he'd ever met.

He dropped the subject, hoping Rhy would be able to knock some sense into her. Yes, it was concerning to know his wife, Devon, was pregnant, but he felt certain the captain of the tactical unit could handle keeping his wife and Alanna safe.

Far better than he could, considering the bounty on his head.

When they'd finished eating breakfast, he set the tray out in the hall, taking a moment to glance around to make sure there was no one lingering nearby. Paranoia came with the job, and he made no apologies for constantly double-checking that they were safe.

He made another pot of coffee, then pulled out his phone. Time to call Lieutenant Harvey.

"What?" Harvey sounded grumpy. Then again, that was his normal demeanor.

"It's Carmichael. I was hoping you'd give me an update." Reed didn't want to ask about the bounty since his buddy had called on the down-low.

"On what? Your case? IA doesn't exactly share their progress with us."

Reed reined in a wave of impatience. "I understand that. But you must have heard something by now. Late last night I helped capture a guy who is likely a member of the Blood Kings. Officer Cohen of the Brookland PD was involved in the arrest. Has anyone questioned the perp? Do we know anything more about Durango's murder?"

"You're on leave, Carmichael. I can't give you information on an active investigation."

It took all his willpower not to shout at his superior officer. "What can you tell me? I'm concerned the Blood Kings will be seeking revenge because I shot and killed Ivan Garcia."

"Okay, okay. Give me a minute. I haven't had any coffee yet," Lieutenant Harvey muttered. Reed heard the sound of fingers clattering on a keyboard. "You should be worried,

Carmichael. The Blood Kings are offering five thousand to anyone who kills you."

He was relieved his boss cared enough to share the news. He injected alarm into his tone. "That's not good, Loo. Other cops will be in danger too. Some of these punks will shoot first and ask questions later."

"I know." Harvey sounded testy. "I can tell you everyone has been put on alert. I just saw the notice myself. We're just getting ready for roll call. According to the message, news of the bounty has been spread across the entire city."

A sudden thought occurred to him. "Are they willing to put me up in a safe house?"

"There's no mention of that, but I'll see what I can do. In the meantime, keep your head down, Carmichael." Harvey's tone was gruff. "The last thing we want is another cop killed in the line of duty."

Like Wesley Durango, he thought.

"I need to know if the guy who broke into Alanna Finnegan's condo has given us any further intel." He frowned as a thought occurred to him. "Do you think he was hoping to get the bounty?"

"I'm not sure. I haven't heard much of anything. Do you have a name?" Harvey asked.

"No, he wouldn't talk. I figure Cohen must have put his prints through the system, though. They probably have an ID on him by now." He'd bet his next paycheck that the guy was a member of the Blood Kings.

"I'll touch base with Cohen and the Brookland PD," Harvey said. "Anything else?"

Plenty, but he sensed he wasn't going to get very far with Lieutenant Harvey. "That's all for now. But I would like to hear any additional information you find out. It's my life on the line here, Loo. I would hope that means something."

"Yeah, yeah. I hear you." There was a pause, then Harvey said, "We're doing roll call. I'll be in touch." With that, he disconnected.

Reed lowered the phone, not at all satisfied with the conversation. Super frustrating that he hadn't learned anything new. He wondered if Harvey would have bothered to call him about the bounty if he hadn't reached out first.

"Rhy and Aiden won't be here for an hour, maybe less." She met his gaze. "I heard you ask about the ID of the guy who broke into my condo. Rhy has the perp's name." She turned her phone so he could see the screen. "Does the name Davonte James mean anything to you?"

"No. May I see that?" He held out his hand for the phone. He shouldn't have been surprised that Rhy had obtained key information on the case before his boss. Rhy probably had connections in every precinct in the city. "How did your brother get this?"

"The homestead is located in Brookland. He knows many of the cops there on a first-name basis."

Remembering how the responding officer had recognized Alanna's last name, he nodded, scanning the series of text messages. "Your brother has already dug into Davonte James's background identifying him as a member of the Blood Kings."

"Yes. We figured that much, right?" Alanna tucked a silky strand of blond hair behind her ear. "According to Officer Cohen, Davonte still isn't talking. They've assigned a public defender to his case. Not sure how long it will take for the lawyer to convince Davonte to cooperate."

Too long, he thought with a grimace. He handed the

phone back to her, not wanting to read all the messages in case they were personal in nature. "I have to say, your family is incredible. They've been more help than the officers in my own district."

Alanna grinned, and he sucked in a breath at how her beautiful features brightened with the force of her smile. "See? Having eight siblings isn't as bad as it sounds."

"I never said that it was bad." He might have thought it, though. Impossible to imagine what her childhood was like compared to his. Chaos was likely putting it mildly. "Knowing your cop brothers are digging into this gives me hope that we'll learn more soon."

"They will." Her tone rang with confidence. "They're good at what they do."

He glanced at the time. "You said less than an hour before they get here?"

"Yeah, sounds like Aiden was able to catch an earlier flight." She consulted her phone, sending off a text. A few seconds later, the phone pinged with a response. "Rhy says they're leaving the homestead in about fifteen minutes. If traffic isn't too bad, they'll be here in within the hour."

He was relieved to hear it. "Great. Do you have all your stuff together? I'd like to head down to the lobby. I remember seeing a computer there that can be used by guests."

"Give me two minutes." Alanna headed into her bedroom. He didn't have a bag, not that it mattered. He'd used the free toothbrush that was in the bathroom, which was all he'd cared about. That and having his backup weapon with ammunition to spare.

Funny how having a price on your head put things into perspective.

When Alanna was ready, he took the duffel from her

fingers and slung it over his shoulder. They walked downstairs to the lobby, waiting in line to do a formal checkout. The hotel was expensive but, in his opinion, money well spent. He left the room charge on his credit card, then headed over to the computer area sitting in a small room off the lobby.

The screen displayed links to various airlines. He opened a search window and typed in the words "Milwaukee Gang Blood Kings."

Several websites came up with the search. Scanning them, he clicked on a news article that had been posted late last night.

"Is that about the shooting in the ED?" Alanna asked, leaning over his shoulder to see the article for herself. She was so close that he could have kissed her by simply turning his head.

Stay focused!

"I—uh, think so." He figured any shooting that took place in the middle of an emergency department would be impossible to keep quiet. Doing his best to ignore Alanna's sweet scent, he scanned the article.

"No mention of your partner who was killed," she whispered. "Why do you think he was left out of the article?"

"I'm sure the brass did their best to cover it up." He was shocked to see that Alanna's name was listed in the article. "Why did they print your full name? That's insane."

"I noticed." She shrugged and straightened. "I guess a member of the medical staff must have given that information to them. I doubt the hospital administrators would have identified me by name."

He couldn't tear his eyes from her name listed in black and white. This was bad. Really bad. Rhy would hit the ceiling when he learned his younger sister had been identified as being involved in the shooting by anyone with access to a newspaper or computer.

And Reed wouldn't blame him for being angry.

He went back to his search on the Blood Kings. Most of the links simply mentioned them as a known gang operating out of Milwaukee. The Latino Hombres were listed too. He clicked several other links, then found one mentioning the local police had formed a task force with the FBI to address the rising gang violence.

That wasn't working too well, was it?

"We should ask Brady about that." Peering over his shoulder again, Alanna tapped the screen. "He may know something."

"We can try." He glanced at his watch, surprised by how much time had passed, then he logged into his email. He took a few more minutes to send a few messages. One to Geoff Watkins and another to his former partner, a guy named Nathan Jackson, to let them both know he may need their help and that he'd be in touch. When he finished, he logged off and stood. "Let's go outside to wait. Your brothers will be here soon."

"Okay." She backed away, giving him room to breathe. Being constantly near her was beginning to wear on him. He admired and cared about her, far more than he should.

He slipped the duffel strap over his shoulder, then headed to the door. Pausing, he scanned the circle drive outside. It was early enough that no one was checking in. And if other guests were checking out, there was no sign of them.

Verifying the circle driveway was empty, he opened the door. "Stay behind me." Normally, he'd let a woman go out first, but safety won over chivalry.

"You're overreacting," Alanna said as they stepped into

the morning sunlight. He hadn't paid attention to the weather, but it appeared they were blessed with a beautiful fall day. The sun shone brightly on the yellow, orange, and red leaves flickering in the trees.

He stood still as two SUVs turned into the parking lot, one right behind the other. He knew without being told that the drivers were Rhy and Aiden.

Finnegans to the rescue.

The thought made him smile, but then he caught a glimpse of movement from his left. He whirled, striking Alanna with the duffel as he withdrew his gun from his holster.

"Hey," she protested, but her comment was cut off by the sound of gunfire.

"Get down!" Reed stepped up, blocking Alanna with his body as he returned fire. The two vehicles raced toward them.

Two men leaped from the SUVs—a redhead he suspected was Aiden and Rhy.

"Get in the car!" Rhy barked.

Aiden rushed forward to grab Alanna's arm. He took her into the second SUV as Rhy joined Reed in pointing his weapon toward the source of the threat.

For long moments, there was nothing but silence. He risked a glance at Rhy. "We need to split up and see if we can find him."

Rhy gave a terse nod. "I'll go right. You take the left."

Reed didn't respond but took off running toward the flash of movement he'd seen. He figured the shooter was long gone, but they needed to know for sure.

The bigger question that flashed neon red in the back of his mind was how members of the Blood Kings had known where to find them.

CHAPTER SIX

"Get down." Aiden none too gently pushed her down to the floor of the back seat of the SUV. Alanna idly wondered where her twin's truck was. Aiden was very fond of his cherry-red truck.

"What's going on?" She tried to lift her head, but Aiden ruthlessly held her down. She fought the urge to bat his arm away.

"Rhy and Reed have split up to find the shooter." Aiden's tense voice did nothing to ease her concern.

"Do you see him?"

"Negative." His clipped tone made him sound as if he were on duty with the National Guard instead of standing in the middle of the circle drive of a suburban hotel. While she'd never seen Aiden in action, she was proud of how determined he was to serve their country.

Seconds ticked by. Finally, she couldn't stand it any longer.

"Let me up. I'm sure he's gone." This time she did shove her brother's arm out of the way to lift her head. Hotel employees peeked through the lobby windows. She suspected the Timberland Falls police would be there any minute.

"They're coming back." Aiden nodded to where Reed and Rhy were jogging toward them. "Guess you're right about the shooter getting away."

"Hop into the SUV," Rhy commanded. "We're getting out of here."

"What about the cops?" On cue, she heard the faint sound of police sirens. "They'll want our statement. And those of the people inside." She gestured toward the lobby doors.

"I'll contact the Timberland Falls Police Department." Rhy waved at the SUV. "Aiden, take them in your vehicle. I'll follow."

"When did you trade your truck in for an SUV?" Alanna settled herself in the back seat while Reed slid in up front.

"It's a rental." Aiden met her gaze in the rearview. "We thought getting you a clean vehicle was for the best."

"Appreciate that," Reed said.

She realized the two men hadn't formally met. "Aiden, this is Reed Carmichael. He works for MPD in district five. Reed, my twin, Aiden."

"Thanks for the backup." Reed gave her brother a nod.

"Anytime." Aiden glanced at Reed. "Rhy filled me in on what happened in the ED last night. We owe you a debt of gratitude for saving Alanna's life."

"Just doing my job." Reed made it clear he wasn't looking for glory.

"I also heard you're on administrative leave for taking out the scumbag who held Alanna hostage." Aiden shook his head. "Frustrating for you, I'm sure."

"It's fine." Reed turned in his seat to look at her. "Did you call anyone while we were at the hotel?"

"No, why?" She thought back. "I texted Rhy, but he called you first, right?"

"You're wondering how the shooter knew your location," Aiden said.

"Exactly." Reed rubbed the back of his neck. "They must have figured it out this morning, or they'd have made an attempt to get to us last night."

"We weren't followed," Aiden said. "If that's what you're thinking."

"I know you weren't. The shooter was already in place when you drove up. I believe he was hunkered down, waiting for us to check out of the hotel."

Waiting for them? She shivered. "I don't understand how the Blood Kings could have uncovered our location."

"I don't either." Reed's tone reeked of frustration. "It doesn't make any sense. We should have been safe there."

"Did you use a credit card?" Aiden asked. "The hotel didn't look like the type that would take cash."

"Yes, but how in the world would a group of gang bangers have the ability to track my credit card?" Reed turned again to look at her. "You didn't talk to anyone at the hospital, right?"

"Correct. I didn't call anyone, and no one called me." She tried not to be irritated that he didn't believe her. "Besides, I doubt anyone from the hospital is involved. They're probably glad I'm off work for a few days. It will provide time for the media circus to settle down."

"I didn't mean to insinuate they were involved." Reed sighed. "I'm just trying to understand what happened."

A phone rang. Her twin pressed the button to take the

call through the dashboard communication system. "What's up, Rhy?"

"I just learned Alanna's full name has been printed in the article about the shooting." Rhy sounded annoyed.

"We just discovered that information this morning too," Reed quickly spoke up. "Trust me, I wasn't happy to see her name either."

"Who did you talk to?" Rhy asked.

"Nobody! I'm not an idiot. I didn't give a single interview, Rhy." She held on to her temper with an effort. "I have no idea who gave out my name. I'm surprised the hospital would do that, considering how strict they are about patient privacy."

"This is not good, sis." Rhy's tone had softened. "We need to meet up to make a plan to ensure your safety moving forward."

"Where do you want to meet?" Reed asked. "I want to make sure Alanna is safe too. We ate breakfast, but if you guys are hungry, we can stop at a restaurant."

"I haven't eaten," Aiden said.

"Okay, we'll head to Rosie's," Rhy said. "You know where the diner is, right?"

"Got it. See you there." Aiden disconnected from the call.

"Have I been to Rosie's?" It didn't sound familiar to her.

"Colin turned us on to it. He claims they have the best breakfasts outside the firehouse." Aiden grinned. "Since those hose jockeys are all about food, I gave the place a try. It's good."

"Hose jockey?" Reed lifted a brow. "You mean firefighter?"

"We also call them smoke eaters," Aiden teased. "We

should call them glorified chefs because they're constantly cooking."

"You're lucky Colin cooks. He's pitched in when Devon was suffering with morning sickness."

"Hey, I gotta give him grief since he took a completely different path than the rest of us." Aiden shook his head. "Not sure what possessed him to go that route."

"Colin puts his life on the line for others just like you do." She felt compelled to defend her brother. "It's not his fault he's a bad shot."

"The worst." Aiden's grin widened. "Good thing he didn't try to join the police academy. They'd have booted him out."

Reed was quiet during their sibling banter, and she knew he was still upset about a gunman showing up at the Timberland Falls Suites. She didn't like it either and couldn't figure out how they'd been found.

"Maybe Rhy will have an idea," she said.

"About what?" Aiden asked.

"How we were found in Timberland Falls." She couldn't see Reed's face but noticed his shoulders were tense. "We might want to contact Brady too. He may know something about the joint MPD and FBI gang task force. Reed read about it while searching online."

"Good idea," Aiden said.

Reed still hadn't said anything, and she found his silence unnerving. The homestead was rarely quiet, even after many of the older sibs had moved out. There was always someone talking or joking around. It was sometimes a game to see who could take the most teasing. So far, Bax was winning out as her brothers had dubbed him penguin, and he'd begun spouting interesting facts about penguins and how great they were, clearly unfazed by the nickname.

Watching Reed now, she hoped he wasn't thinking of a way to ditch her. No doubt wanting to force her to go with her family.

"Aiden, will you stop at an ATM?" Reed's voice broke into her thoughts.

"Sure. You need cash?"

"Yeah." Reed didn't expound on his plans.

"There's a limit as to how much you can remove at a time," she pointed out. "I'll pull out some cash too."

"I can do the same," Aiden offered.

Reed's jaw tensed, but he nodded in agreement. "Thanks."

Yep, there was no doubt in her mind he was planning to ditch her. And she almost wished Aiden hadn't returned early from his training. Reed would assume, rightly, that she'd be safe enough with Aiden watching over her.

There had to be a way to convince him they needed to stick together.

Aiden exited the freeway, navigating through side streets to reach Rosie's Diner. When they passed a bank nearby, he pulled over so they could all withdraw cash. Once they'd each removed two hundred dollars, they climbed back into the rental.

The diner was just a few blocks away. Aiden pulled in and parked. Glancing behind her, she could see Rhy behind the wheel of the SUV turning into the parking lot behind them.

Rosie's Diner was packed, but a group of four people stood to leave as they entered. Aiden pushed forward to grab the booth. She and Reed followed. Seconds later, Rhy stepped inside to join them.

Her brothers took the seat across from her and Reed. She was hyperaware of Reed's closeness and hoped her feelings weren't evident on her features. Thankfully, her brothers focused on the menu as a server came over with coffee. She'd already downed plenty but accepted the mug anyway. No doubt, this would be another long day.

"Did you talk to the Timberland Falls police?" She eyed Rhy over the rim of her cup.

"Yeah." He shrugged. "They're not happy we left the scene but reluctantly took my statement over the phone. I told them I'd have you both call to provide your statements too." Her brother pinned her and Reed with a solemn gaze. "I'll text Detective North's contact information to both of you."

"That's fine." Reed still hadn't said much, giving no indication of what he was thinking. She took a sip of her coffee and added, "We need to find a place to stay where we can fly under the radar."

Rhy arched a brow. "You're talking like a cop, sis. Reed must be rubbing off on you."

"Really? You're going to blame Reed? I grew up surrounded by cops." She narrowed her gaze. "You, Tarin, Brady, and Kyleigh have rubbed off on me."

Their server came to take their order. She and Reed refrained from anything other than coffee, while Aiden ordered the largest breakfast Rosie offered. Rhy ordered a short stack of pancakes.

"Aiden needs to take Alanna somewhere safe." Reed spoke for the first time. "I'd like her kept under wraps until this mess with the Blood Kings has been resolved."

"And leave you alone?" She turned in her seat to glare at him. "Not happening. You need protection more than I do."

"She's right, Reed," Rhy drawled. "Seems like both of you are in the kill zone."

"Listen to me." Reed leaned forward, his voice low and earnest. "I have no idea who I can trust. There's no reason to drag Alanna along for this ride. I'm sure no one will get through the Finnegan family wall of protection."

She knew Reed was anxious to get rid of her, but his statement still stung. More than it should. She lifted her chin. "Those guys came to my condo. And my name is in the paper. I think that means we're both equally in danger. All the more reason we need to stick together."

"She has a point," Rhy said.

"No, she doesn't," Reed snapped. Then sighed. "I mean, yes, she's in danger, but Aiden seems more than capable of keeping her safe. I can handle staying under the radar alone."

"And do what?" Rhy asked. "You can't investigate the Blood Kings yourself, not when you have a bounty on your head."

"I'll figure it out." Reed dug in his heels, refusing to budge. "You don't need to worry about me. You should be focused on your sister."

"I'm worried about you!" The comment came out louder than she'd intended, and several café patrons glanced over at their table. She lowered her voice. "Don't be a knucklehead, Reed. My cop brothers won't leave you hanging in the wind."

"She's right," Aiden said. The conversation paused as their server brought their food in record time. "We need to contact Brady."

"Why is that?" Rhy asked with a frown.

"Because there's a joint task force between MPD and the FBI to combat the rising crime related to gang activity," Reed explained.

"Okay, I'll give him a call. First, we'll say grace." Rhy

bowed his head, and the rest of them followed suit. "Dear Lord Jesus, we are thankful for the food You've provided for us. We ask that You continue to keep Reed and Alanna safe in Your care. Amen."

"Amen." She darted a look at Reed, noting he didn't look uncomfortable with the prayer the way her previous boyfriends had. Especially Dom. She should have known dating a doctor was a bad idea. Hadn't she noticed how many of the residents flirted with the nurses? Even the married ones? Dominic might have been handsome, but she'd soon learned monogamy wasn't his strong suit.

Rhy took a bite of his pancake, then pulled his phone from his pocket. "The next step is to find a safe place for both of you. Brady might have a place in mind too."

Reed shot her a frustrated look. She met his stare head-on, unwilling to back down. If he thought he was going to shake her off that easily, he was dead wrong.

After the way he'd saved her life, she had no intention of letting him deal with this on his own. He might not know what it was like to have a big family, but he'd learn.

They were all in this together.

REED COULDN'T UNDERSTAND why Alanna was pushing so hard for them to stay together. She had ten stitches in her throat courtesy of the Blood Kings and had narrowly escaped being shot not just once, but several times.

Her brothers should be wrapping her in cotton and sticking her someplace safe for the next week at the very least. That's what he would do if he wasn't being targeted by an entire bloodthirsty gang of Blood Kings.

"Brady, it's Rhy. Call me. Alanna's in a dangerous situation, and we need your help." Rhy lowered his phone to the table. "I'm sure he'll call when he can."

Reed had no doubt that using Alanna's name would garner a quick response. He sat back in the booth, eyeing the Finnegans seated across from him. There had to be some way to convince them to take Alanna under their wing, leaving him to find his own way through this mess. "Does Brady have access to FBI safe houses?"

"Possibly." Rhy shrugged. "Not sure you and Alanna will qualify for one if he has to go through official channels."

Aiden groaned when his phone buzzed. He pulled it from his pocket. "I gotta take this." He stood and left the diner, raising the phone to his ear.

Reed had a bad feeling that Aiden was being called back to work. Rhy's gaze mirrored his thoughts. In that moment, he understood their concern was primarily for their sister and that he was expected to help protect her.

"Did he leave his training early because of me?" Alanna demanded. "I told you not to call him."

"He called me," Rhy said. "And yeah, I mentioned how you were hurt by a gang member. He made it sound like he could leave without getting in trouble."

"And you believed him?" Alanna rolled her eyes.

Reed set his coffee down. It had grown cold anyway. "If Brady can't come up with a safe house, maybe we can rent something. It would be better if the rental wasn't in my name, though."

"So now we are sticking together?" Alanna asked.

"If that's what your brothers think is best." He caught the flash of gratitude in Rhy's gaze and knew he was sunk.

Aiden was still outside talking on the phone. When he returned a few minutes later, his expression was pained.

"Looks like I won't be able to stay in town after all. A tornado touched down in Alabama last night, hitting a hospital. We're deploying in six hours."

"Understandable," Rhy said. "Don't worry, we'll make sure Alanna is safe."

Aiden pinned Reed with a look. "And you'll protect her too. Right?"

"With my life." Reed knew there was no backing out now.

Rhy plucked his phone off the table. It took Reed a minute to realize the device had been in silent mode when the screen lit up with Brady's name. "Hey, did you see the article about Alanna being held hostage in the ED?"

Just hearing the words took Reed back to those heart-wrenching moments when he'd been forced to shoot Ivan Garcia. Alanna's shoulder brushed his, making him wish he could put his arm around her.

"What do you know about a joint task force to address gang violence?" Rhy asked. There were long moments of silence while he listened to Brady's response. Then Rhy said, "Any chance you have a safe house we can use?"

Rhy's grim expression indicated the answer was no. Reed pulled out his phone and searched for rental properties. He didn't dare book it under his name or credit card, but he knew the Finnegans would take care of it once he found a place. It didn't take long, and he turned his phone toward Rhy who nodded.

"Okay, we have a place in mind," Rhy said. "We'd like to meet up with you later. I'll text you the address." Another pause, then he said, "Thanks, bro."

"Where are we headed?" Alanna asked.

Reed showed her the two-bedroom house he'd found.

"It's not too expensive. But I need someone else to book the place so my name isn't associated with it."

"I'll do it." Aiden took the phone from his hand, looked at the place, then used his phone to make the arrangements.

"Thanks, Aiden. I can pay you back." Alanna smiled at her twin. "I know you're saving for a house."

"It's fine. I'm glad to chip in since I can't stick around long enough to cover your six." Aiden truly looked disappointed at having to leave. "There. You're all set for the next two days. You can extend your stay longer if you need to, but I didn't want to lock you in any longer than necessary."

Reed thought that was smart since he still didn't understand how they'd been found in Timberland Falls. He trusted the Finnegans, but his mind kept going back to the call he'd received from his buddy at the precinct. Had the call been a ruse? A way to track his cell phone to the Timberland Falls Suites? He didn't want to believe any of his fellow cops were dirty, especially stooping so low as to mingle with gang bangers.

Yet after thinking through everything that had happened, that was the only call that could have resulted in betraying their location.

He wouldn't make that mistake again. And if he couldn't call the precinct, his ability to get inside information was limited.

As Rhy and Aiden finished their respective meals, he said, "I took two calls last night. One from you, Rhy. And one from a fellow officer in my district, Chuck Simmons. He called to let me know about the Blood Kings putting a bounty on my head." He met Rhy's gaze. "Now I'm wondering if he set me up."

"It seems a stretch to think a cop would sell out a

brother in blue over a measly five grand," Rhy said. "You didn't make any other calls?"

"One after breakfast to Lieutenant Harvey. Even harder to believe he's responsible."

"Maybe not Harvey himself, but he could have mentioned your call to someone else." Rhy shoved his empty plate away. "All the more reason for you and Alanna to stay together. We'll be your conduit for information from this point forward."

He nodded, grateful to have Rhy's understanding. "We should get rid of our phones, too, then. Get cheap throw-away devices instead."

"I can grab those for you," Aiden offered. He grin faded. "After that, I need to leave."

"Hey, I'm glad you were here for a short while." Alanna reached across the table to touch her twin's hand. "You always seem to sense when I'm in danger. Remember how you barged into my dorm room when Kurt got all handsy with me?"

"Jerk," Aiden muttered.

Reed silently echoed Aiden's assessment. He was glad Alanna had her twin brother nearby when she'd needed him.

Rhy signaled the server for their tab. Reed wished he could offer to pay, but he wanted to keep as much cash on hand as possible on the off chance they had to go on the run again.

From this point forward, he'd be prepared for the worst-case scenario, no matter what.

The gunfire outside the hotel was proof that he couldn't underestimate the power of the bounty on his head. And the thirst for revenge from the rest of the Blood Kings.

"Let's go." Rhy paid the tab, then pushed at Aiden to get

him out of the booth. "I'll feel better once we have Reed and Alanna stashed somewhere safe."

"Safety is an illusion," Alanna muttered. He slipped out of the booth, then gestured for her to follow Aiden so he could stay behind her.

Rhy paused at the door, glancing around the parking lot for a moment before crossing the threshold. Aiden went next, holding the door for his twin.

Reed stayed close to Alanna as they headed toward the SUVs parked next to each other. Aiden turned to glance at him. "Take the keys." He tossed them into the air for Reed to catch. "I'll ride with Rhy. We'll pick up the phones and meet you at the house."

"Understood." The word had barely left his mouth when he heard the crack of gunfire. He jumped forward, covering Alanna with his body and pulling her toward the relative safety of the SUV.

"Go!" Rhy barked. "Get her out of here."

Aiden had pulled his weapon and returned fire. Rhy had his weapon in hand too. Reed wanted to help back them up, but he had the keys to the SUV, and asking Alanna to leave on her own wasn't an option.

He yanked open the driver's side door and pushed Alanna inside. "Keep your head down as you get up and over the console."

As soon as she'd cleared the driver's seat, he slid in behind the wheel. Seconds later, he started the engine and shot backward out of the parking spot. The gunfire abruptly stopped as each party tried to find the other.

"Go!" Rhy shouted.

He hit the gas and sped away from Rosie's Diner, fingers tight on the steering wheel. How on earth did the gang members find them? He knew the Finnegans would never betray their sister, so the information must have come from some other source.

He abruptly turned, heading for the freeway rather than the house Aiden had secured for them.

Time for plan B.

CHAPTER SEVEN

When would this madness stop? Alanna gripped the passenger-side door with cramped fingers. "How?" Her voice was little more than a croak. "How did they find us?"

Reed slowly shook his head. "I don't know." When they were on the interstate, he lowered his window and chucked his phone out.

She stared in shock. "You believe they tracked your phone to find us at Rosie's?"

"Yeah." He didn't elaborate, and a chill snaked down her spine. "Turn your phone off for now. We'll find a place where you can use it to arrange a meeting with your brothers."

Unclamping her fingers from the door handle, she fished her phone from her pocket and powered it down. She stared at the black screen for a long minute. "Is it safe to do that? To call my family?"

"I'm the one with a bounty on my head. Not you." His expression twisted into a grimace. "I wish you would stay with your family, Alanna. I'm too big of a target."

She was weary of repeating the same arguments. "Are you heading to the rental Aiden arranged?"

"Not yet." He glanced at her. "I trust your family, but what if a cop is involved in this? I think any cop on the force would figure out Rhy and Tarin are helping us."

"Aiden wasn't even supposed to be home," she pointed out. "I doubt anyone would think to look for his name on a vacation rental."

"We've been found twice in a matter of hours." Reed's tone was clipped. "I'm not taking any chances. Not with your life."

And she wasn't about to risk his either, she silently agreed. "Okay, then who can we get to make arrangements for us?"

"I'm not sure who I can trust." He looked so dejected her heart hurt.

She was about to offer her sister Kyleigh as an option but then remembered how her sister and husband were all over the news back in March when Kyleigh shot and killed T-Turbo, a famous musician who had been on trial for murder. "We can ask one of the Callahans for help. Dana Callahan was in the ED the night Ivan Garcia held me hostage. We could also ask Maddy Sinclair to make arrangements. Her husband, Noah, is on the job too."

He hesitated, considering the two options. Finally, he nodded. "I've always liked working for Noah. But rather than go with another cop from my precinct, it would be better to talk to Maddy Sinclair. I know the DA's office often uses hotels for witnesses that come in from out of town. Maybe an arrangement made by the DA's office wouldn't stand out as unusual."

"Okay. I'll call my sister Elly when you deem it safe

enough to use my phone. Elly has Maddy's personal contact information."

"They're friends?" Reed asked.

"Friends and cousins. Maddy and Elly were the ones who found the DNA connection." She frowned realizing Elly hadn't given them an update on the status of the family tree. "Apparently, our grandmothers were sisters. But somehow they lost touch when our Finnegan grandmother left when she was sixteen. We don't know what happened, but I know Maddy and Elly were both looking into it."

He nodded, his intense gaze so focused on the road she doubted he'd paid much attention. That was okay, he had more important issues on his mind than understanding their family tree and what may have held the sisters apart so many years ago.

After ten minutes, he exited the freeway. "What do you think about going to see Maddy in person? Rather than calling?"

"Ah, sure. Although she could be in court. I know from Kyleigh the ADAs spend a fair amount of time there in various hearings. Even if there isn't an impending trial."

"We'll take a chance. If she's not there, maybe we can wait for her if she's not tied up too long." He seemed determined not to leave an electronic trail, and based on the way they'd been found over and over again, she couldn't blame him.

"If my brother-in-law is there, we can use his landline phone to call my brothers."

"I like that plan." His fingers seemed to relax a bit on the steering wheel. He glanced at her. "I'm sorry to be so paranoid."

"No need to apologize." She managed a reassuring

smile, doing her best to remain positive despite the nerve-racking danger. "This will work, you'll see."

Reed gave a slight nod. A few minutes later, he pulled into the underground parking garage beneath McArthur Park next to the courthouse. She led the way up the stairs to the main level. The ADA's office wasn't far from the courthouse, so she turned in that direction.

"Not many people around," he murmured, resting one hand in the small of her back.

"It's early. Soon this place will be crawling with people. The courthouse opens at eight a.m., but most cases don't start until nine."

The trek to the administrative building didn't take long. The main door was open, but from there they had to speak to a receptionist. She stepped forward to take the lead. "I'm looking for either Bax Scala or Maddy Sinclair."

"Do you have an appointment?" The woman gave them a dubious look. "They are both very busy."

"No, but if you could let them know that Alanna Finnegan is here, that would be great." She caught the flash of recognition in the receptionist's eyes. "Bax is my brother-in-law, and Maddy is my cousin."

"One moment please." She picked up a phone and spoke in low tones to someone on the other end. Thirty seconds later, she replaced the receiver and gestured toward the door. "Both Bax and Maddy are in their offices."

"Thank you." Alanna crossed over as Reed quickly followed, leaning forward to grab the door for her.

"Have you been here before?" he asked.

"Only once." She sent him a bemused smile. "I usually don't have to deal with the DA's office. Kyleigh brought me here once when we met Bax for lunch. I know Maddy by name but never met her in person."

"There's Maddy's office." Reed nodded at the name-plate outside the first door on the right.

She knocked. "Maddy? It's Alanna Finnegan."

"Come in." Maddy rose, greeting them with a wide smile. "It's great to see you, Alanna. I've heard so much about you from Dana."

"Thanks, oh, this is Reed Carmichael. He's an MPD cop."

Reed shook Maddy's hand. "I haven't been to the offices here, but I've seen you in the courthouse."

"Yes, we know how much the officers love to come down to testify for us," Maddy teased. She gestured to her chairs. "Please sit. I don't have much time, unfortunately. What do you need from me?"

"A favor." She decided to get straight to the point. "Noah may have told you about Reed's situation. The Blood Kings are out to kill him and have offered a five-thousand-dollar reward for anyone who does the deed."

Maddy's gaze sharpened. "I know, it's terrible, and highly unusual. Gangs generally avoid killing cops."

"I killed Ivan 'Ice' Garcia when he was holding Alanna hostage. I suspect they're making an exception in this case."

"So scary." Maddy's blue eyes captured hers. "I'm glad you weren't hurt worse."

"Me too." Alanna knew time was running short. "We don't want to keep you too long, but the bottom line is that we have been found several times by gunmen. We need you to make arrangements for us to stay in a hotel that can't be traced back to either of us."

"Of course." Maddy didn't hesitate. She picked up her phone and spoke to someone else. "I need a two-bedroom suite at the City Central Hotel starting immediately with no estimated date of leaving. Thanks, Jennifer." She replaced the receiver. "We use the City Central Hotel for most of our witnesses. This will hopefully appear to be yet another witness being housed there for the DA's office."

"Great, thank you." She rose to her feet. "We need to talk to Bax too."

"He's right down the hall." Maddy stood. "I'm sorry I can't stay; judges get cranky when ADAs are late for court." Her gaze turned somber. "Please be careful. Both of you. I know what it's like to be in danger. I'll pray for your safety."

"Thank you." It was tempting to hug her cousin, and maybe her gratitude showed because Maddy enveloped her in a hug.

"Be safe," Maddy murmured as they turned to leave. Maddy grabbed her briefcase and followed them out.

"That was amazing," Reed said in a low voice. "She never hesitated to offer her assistance."

"I know." She couldn't help but smile. "Families are great."

"Alanna?" Hearing Bax, she moved forward. He held a briefcase, too, as if he was also heading to court. "What's up? Do you need something?"

"Hi, Bax." She gave him a quick hug. "This is Reed Carmichael. We don't want to keep you, but can we borrow your phone to make a quick call?"

"Of course." He gestured toward his office. "Cell or landline?"

"Landline," Reed said. "If that's okay."

She brushed past Bax to reach the desk. She quickly dialed Rhy's cell number. He answered on the first ring. "Where are you? We're finishing up here at the diner."

"Reed dumped his phone, and I shut mine down too. We still need new phones but have a different location in mind." Aware of the fact that she was keeping Bax from court, she quickly gave Rhy the information. "We'll talk more when you get to City Central, okay? Bax has court."

"Later," Rhy agreed.

She hung up the phone, then hurried out of the office to find Reed filling Bax in on the danger. Her brother-in-law glanced at her in concern. "I hope Rhy is aware of this."

"He is." She gestured with her hand. "Let's walk. I don't want you to be late."

"Using the City Central Hotel is a good idea," Bax said as they exited the administrative building. "I would have made the arrangements for you."

"I know, but we thought Maddy was at least one step removed from the Finnegan family."

"I'll make sure she gets reimbursed," Bax said.

"I'll settle up with all payments made on our behalf once this is over," Reed said in a firm tone.

"No need, I'm happy to donate to the cause." Alanna knew Bax didn't care much about money. Maybe because he had a nice inheritance that he'd gotten from his Italian grandparents. "Besides, it sounds like that's the least of your worries. Keep your head down, and you too, Alanna."

"We will." She did her best to sound confident. "Reed has excellent instincts when it comes to keeping us safe."

Reed scowled but didn't say anything more. When they reached the corner, Bax turned toward the courthouse. "Take care, both of you."

"Thanks, Bax." After waiting for the light to change, she caught Reed's hand and led the way across the street, the opposite direction from the courthouse. "I think the City Central Hotel is this way."

"I don't like the idea of leaving the car in the parking garage," Reed said in a low voice. "The only way to pay is with a debit or credit card."

"We'll get my brothers to take care of it." She tightened her grip on his fingers. "It's a short walk to the hotel. We'll be fine."

He nodded, his gaze moving from side to side as he scanned their surroundings. She didn't see how anyone from the Blood Kings could know their location. Then again, she'd had the same thought about the hotel in Timberland Falls. That hadn't turned out so well.

They made it to City Central without incident. Once inside, they approached the front desk. She smiled at the clerk. "We're here for the two-bedroom suite arranged by the DA's office."

"Ah, yes. Here you go." The desk clerk slid two keys across the counter without asking for any form of ID. For the first time since leaving Rosie's Diner, she felt Reed relax beside her. "Your room is on the first floor, down that hallway." She gestured with her hand to a hallway that seemed to run behind the desk and office area.

"Thank you." She handed Reed a key. Without saying anything more, they took the hallway, finding the two-bedroom suite without difficulty.

She unlocked the door and stepped inside. The room wasn't nearly as nice as the one they'd stayed in last night, but it would work well enough.

Reed sighed, rubbed the back of his neck, then walked through the room toward the bedrooms. Without saying anything more, he went into the room and closed the door behind him.

Alanna dropped onto the worn sofa, unsure what she could say or do to make Reed feel better. It seemed outrageous to think anyone from within the police department could possibly be involved with scum like the Blood Kings.

They were safe here. But the bigger question remained:

How would they get out of this mess? It seemed like the only way to end this nightmare was to arrest every single member of the Blood Kings.

A seemingly impossible endeavor.

REED sluiced cold water on his face, struggling to remain calm. He didn't want Alanna to be anywhere near him and the giant red target on his back, yet her connections with the DA's office had proved invaluable.

Bracing his hands on either side of the sink, he took several deep breaths. Bad enough that his being there put Alanna in danger, but he had no idea what he could do to bring an end to this nightmare.

Sitting around and waiting for his fellow officers to find and arrest the leader of the Blood Kings was hardly an option.

So was talking to anyone in his precinct. He didn't want any more gunmen crawling from the woodwork.

Enough. He straightened and gave himself a narrow glare. This helplessness wasn't like him. Alanna's brothers would be there soon with replacement phones. Maybe they would have some ideas.

He was fresh out of them at the moment.

As he made his way back to the living area, he thought about how the Finnegans leaned on their faith in times like this. He swallowed hard and lifted his gaze to the ceiling.

Lord, I know I don't deserve Your grace, but Alanna does. Please keep her safe.

Feeling better, he crossed over to the sofa where Alanna sat, staring down at the thin carpeting. "Are you okay?"

"Yes." She glanced up at him. "How are you?"

"I'm fine." He grimaced. "I hate feeling helpless. It's bugging me that I don't have anyone inside my district that I can trust."

"You can trust the Finnegans and the Callahans." She rested her hand on his knee. "We'll get through this."

Here she was, ten stitches in her neck yet reassuring him that they would be all right. "I know." He covered her hand with his. "We need a plan, though. Something we can do to figure out who is behind this."

"You mean besides the entire Blood Kings gang?" Her gaze was wry. "How many people is that anyway? Do you know?"

"No clue." He stared at their joined hands. "I keep going back to my partner's murder. And the way his body was placed in our squad." The image of the rookie's dead eyes staring up at him flashed in his memory. "He must have been killed before Garcia grabbed you, or he would have been in the ambulance. I'm trying to understand how anyone from the Blood Kings knew that I shot Garcia in time to stick Durango's body in our squad?"

"Don't forget there were two gang members who came to help Garcia escape." She sucked in a harsh breath. "Maybe they're the same ones who put Wesley in the car?"

"Maybe, but Garcia was still alive then." Reed couldn't quite put his finger on the piece of the puzzle that nagged at him. "They couldn't have known I'd be the one who would take him out."

"Maybe choosing your squad was a coincidence?" Alanna suggested.

"I generally don't believe in them." He shook his head. "At least, not when it comes to police work."

"That's what my brothers say too." She sighed. "Who else was at the initial shooting scene that night?"

"A lot of cops responded, some from outside our district." He frowned, then abruptly stood, glancing around for paper and pen. Spying a small notepad near the phone on the desk, he quickly strode over to take a seat. "It's a good idea to make a list."

He was halfway through his list when there was a knock at the door. Alanna waved him back. "I'll get it."

"Check who it is," he cautioned, although he didn't need to. She went up on her tiptoes to peer through the spy hole before opening the door.

"Hey, Rhy. Where's Aiden?"

"I dropped him off at the homestead." Rhy had a laptop under his arm and carried a plastic bag.

"You brought a computer?" He rose. "That's perfect."

"This isn't our first rodeo." Rhy set the computer on the desk, then handed the bag to Alanna. "Two disposable phones. And some extra cash. Normally I'd bring spare weapons, but Reed is already armed, and I didn't think you'd want a gun."

"I don't. Thanks, Rhy." She rummaged in the bag. "I'll get the phones set up."

"Yes, I need both numbers." Rhy dropped onto the sofa. "Brady will be here soon."

Reed glanced at Alanna's brother. "Did he know about the task force?"

"Yes, but unfortunately, he hasn't been involved." Rhy shrugged. "He's digging for information and will share what he knows when he gets here. By the way, smart move asking Bax to set up the room for you through the DA's office."

"Actually, it was Maddy Sinclair that had her assistant make the arrangements." Alanna grinned. "I only used Bax's phone to call you."

Rhy arched a brow. "Maybe that was for the best. Maddy is less likely to lead back to you."

"That was the goal." He opened the computer. "Hey, this looks new."

"It is new," Rhy said. "Don't worry, I paid cash."

The Finnegan generosity was a bit overwhelming. "I'll pay you back."

Rhy waved a hand. "No biggie. It's better to stay focused on these idiot gunmen who are determined to kill you."

He turned to face him. "Did you catch the guy outside Rosie's Diner?"

"One of my men did." Rhy smiled. "Joe Kingsley grabbed him. The shooter babbled about the reward, but from what Joe has told me, he doesn't have any gang tats. We're thinking he's a Blood Kings wannabe."

"Not all of them are inked up," he protested. "Maybe he is part of the Blood Kings."

"Maybe. He's in jail and being held without bond due to charges of attempting to kill a police officer, along with illegal possession of a firearm." Rhy held his gaze. "Since the shooting took place in a different district than the one you work out of, I'm hoping the guy talks to save his own skin."

"That would be great, but I won't hold my breath. These gang members don't rat each other out very often."

"You'd think they would in order to avoid prolonged jail time," Alanna said with a frown.

"Many of the jails are run with the same street-gang mentality." Rhy sighed. "If he does rat out the Blood Kings, and there are other Blood Kings in the same cell block he is? His life wouldn't be worth much."

"Exactly. Which is why it's rare for them to give out useful info. Yet it's possible this guy is young enough to make a mistake." Reed glanced at his list. "I keep going back to the original shooting that caused all of this. I'm making a list of the cops I remember who were at the scene."

Rhy leaned forward, his gaze intense. "You think one of them is working with the Blood Kings?"

"My partner was somehow taken from the initial scene and subsequently murdered. At first, I assumed a few of the gang members managed to grab him as a random hostage. But after these recent shooting incidents, I can't help but think they have inside help." It pained him to think a cop would do something like this. Yet he couldn't come up with another scenario where his calls to the precinct would result in gunmen finding them.

"I see what you mean." Rhy looked equally grim. "Hopefully, Brady will have additional insight."

He nodded but didn't have much hope of learning anything about a possible crooked cop from a task force. He turned back to his list, racking his brain to remember everyone he'd seen.

He had to admit, there were likely officers he'd missed. Impossible to take note of everyone, especially knee-deep in chaos.

When he'd finished his list, he only had eight names. Eight sounded like a lot, but he felt sure he'd missed a few. He thought about the emails he'd sent to both Geoff Watkins and his former partner, Nate Jackson. He quickly checked his email for a response, but there was nothing.

Which was odd. He was close to both of them. Even though Nate had left his precinct after getting married, they'd often kept in touch.

Rhy's phone rang. "Brady? We're here. Thanks." He lowered his phone. "Brady is in the parking lot."

"That reminds me, the rental SUV is in the underground parking garage," Alanna said. "We didn't want to risk using our debit or credit card."

"I'll take care of it." Rhy crossed over to the door, looking through the peephole. A few minutes later, he opened the door. "Thanks for coming, Brady."

"Of course." Brady's gaze zeroed in on Alanna's stitches. "That looks rough, sis."

"I'm fine." She went over to hug her brother, then turned to face him. "This is Reed Carmichael. He's the cop who shot Ivan Garcia and saved my life."

"We owe you a debt of gratitude." Brady's expression was grave as they shook hands. "Those of us in law enforcement are well aware of the danger of being on the front lines. I don't think any of us expected Alanna to be taken hostage in the middle of her shift."

"I was just doing my job." Reed tried to smile, but it felt strained. "I was glad to be there in time. Unfortunately, your sister has been in danger ever since. And that's on me."

"That's on the Blood Kings," Rhy corrected. "We don't blame you, Carmichael."

They should, and if the situation was reversed, Reed wasn't sure he'd be so cavalier about it. He refocused his gaze on the fed. "Do you have anything you can tell us that will help get to the bottom of this mess?"

"I spoke to a member of the task force." Brady pulled the desk chair over. Reed sat beside Alanna on the sofa, while Rhy took the other chair. "He claims they've been working with snitches to get names of gang members, but that it's been slow going."

"Any indication a cop is involved?" Alanna asked.

Brady's eyes widened. "No, why? You think there is?"

"Yes, but it's a long story." Reed stood and grabbed the list of officers he'd been able to remember from the scene.

He handed it to Brady. "Can you tell me if anyone on this list is on the task force?"

Brady scanned the names. "Yes, this guy, Officer Tate Brown is on the task force."

Tate Brown. Reed glanced at Rhy, who nodded as if reading his mind. "Well, I guess that's the place to start."

It was the first lead they'd had since the beginning of this mess. Reed only hoped it would lead them to the head of the Blood Kings gang.

Before it was too late.

CHAPTER EIGHT

"Officer Tate Brown?" Alanna glanced between Reed and her brothers. "You believe he's dirty because he's working on the task force?" The logic escaped her.

"Not necessarily," Reed quickly said. "But he's on the task force and was at the scene of the gang shooting. I don't think it's a stretch to think he may know something. Maybe even saw something related to my partner's murder."

"He'd have gone through channels if he did," Rhy said with a frown. "At least, he should have."

Reed shrugged. "Even if he did, the upper brass won't let me know about it. Not while I'm on administrative leave."

"I'll reach out to him," Brady offered.

"Which fed is on the task force?" Reed asked. "You said it's not you, so it must be someone else."

Brady hesitated, then said, "Our DEA agent, Doug Bridges. I know him pretty well. He was shot back in July." Brady's gaze cut to Rhy. "You remember the incident with Quinn and Sami."

"I do." Rhy grimaced. "That was a tough one. I didn't realize he was back on full duty."

"Only since early September," Brady said. "He was offered the chance to retire early but wanted to stay on the job."

"He's dedicated," Rhy murmured.

Reed looked confused, so Alanna filled him in. "My brother Quinn works for the Coast Guard. Sami was an undercover cop working for the DEA related to drugs being transported through the Great Lakes. The drug cartel had infiltrated the FBI, and the agent in charge set up Agent Bridges. The cartel members kidnapped Sami intending to kill her. Agent Bridges was shot during the scuffle."

Reed's eyebrows hiked upward. "You Finnegans sure get yourselves in dicey situations."

"You have no idea," Rhy said with a sigh.

"Part of the job." Brady waved a hand. "Back to the issue at hand, the feeling among law enforcement was that there were less drugs coming in after the takedown and arrest of the dirty cops involved. At least the Robles cartel wasn't operating here as much. But now there's been another spike in drugs and illegal arms, several busts linked back to an increase in gang activity. Hence the task force."

"The focus of the group is drugs?" Reed asked.

"No, the focus is mainly on gang violence, but you know as well as I do that the root of that concern is drugs and guns, with a little prostitution thrown in. The good news is that Doug Bridges is a friend. He'll share information without a problem."

"Okay, when can we start?" Alanna was thrilled to have something constructive to do. Sitting around wasn't the norm. When the disposable phones were charged and ready to go, she handed one to Reed. "Do you think Agent Bridges will meet with us?"

"I'll call him." Brady stood and headed to one of the bedrooms where he could make the call in private.

"What about you, Rhy?" Reed held her brother's gaze. "Don't you have to go? I'm sure you're supposed to be at work."

"I took the day off." Rhy acted as if it wasn't a big deal, but Alanna frowned.

"Does that mean you'll have one less day of vacation to use when the baby is born?" She gave him a narrow look. "Devon won't appreciate that."

"Devon understands family comes first." Reed offered a gentle smile. "Besides, this one day won't impact my time off. I have been banking all my personal days for a while now. Devon and I agreed that we won't use them all right away, regardless. We want additional time off over the holidays."

She was only slightly mollified. "I still think you shouldn't take the entire day off for me."

"Always for you, or the other sibs." Rhy leaned over to pat her knee. "I promise this isn't a big deal."

She hoped he was right but doubted it. Ever since their parents died when she and Aiden were seventeen, Rhy had worried about her. Aiden and Elly, too, but mostly the youngest sisters. The entire family had been relieved when Rhy had fallen in love with Devon. It had been well past time for him to live his own life.

Marrying Devon and starting a family was a great start, but he didn't have to continue worrying about the rest of them. They were all adults now, even Elly. Although the youngest still didn't seem settled in her role as an EMT.

"Doug Bridges is on his way," Brady announced, interrupting her thoughts. "He's not sure how much help he can be, but he's willing to pitch in."

"He was instrumental in supporting Quinn and Sami," Rhy said. "I still feel guilty about how he was injured helping to protect them."

"Part of the job, remember?" Brady's expression turned serious. "I mentioned Officer Tate Brown. He doesn't know much about the guy. I figure we can dig into his past a bit."

Having a lead was proving anticlimactic. Alanna shifted in her seat, wishing they could do something instead of sitting around talking about the case. She glanced at Reed, who appeared relaxed and calm. Maybe she was the only impatient one.

"Not all police work is hitting the streets." He seemed to read her thoughts. "Pouring through details is important too."

"I understand." She blew out a long, slow breath. Rhy was always talking about the prep work involved prior to implementing a tactical situation. And she knew Tarin spent a lot of time digging into victims and suspects too.

Maybe this was another reason she'd chosen nursing, especially a fast-paced environment like the emergency department. Even before the pandemic, there was no shortage of patients seeking medical care. And that number had grown exponentially in the years since.

"Give me your new cell numbers," Brady said.

"I need them as well," Rhy added.

It only took a minute to get her number and Reed's listed in her brothers' phones. She put their numbers in her phone and Reed's as well. "We're all set." For what, she wasn't sure.

"Good. I'm heading down to the lobby to meet Bridges."

Brady strode to the door. "I didn't give him much information over the phone."

Alanna took that to mean her brother hadn't shared the full extent of the danger she and Reed were in. She scooted closer to Reed. He took her hand in a reassuring gesture.

Thankfully, Rhy didn't seem to notice, his gaze focused on his phone. "Excuse me." He stood and moved away. "Hey, Dev. How are you?"

"I wish Rhy would go home," she whispered. "Devon is due the middle of next month, and I would hate for her to be stressed over Rhy being involved in this."

"Maybe once Bridges arrives, he'll feel safer leaving." Reed squeezed her hand. "Your family is something special."

"They are." She managed a smile. "Sometimes too nosy, butting into each other's private business, but super supportive just the same."

"I don't blame Rhy for the way he looks out for you. Brady too." Reed's expression turned serious. "I really wish you'd go home with them, Alanna. There's no reason for you to stay here with me."

"Give it up, Reed." Her tone was sharper than she'd intended. "My name in the paper means I'm staying. And you know my brothers will continue helping too."

"That part is incredible, but it doesn't mean the two are mutually exclusive. I would feel better knowing you were safe."

She sighed. "I'm safe here with you. Drop it, okay? Let's move on."

Reed twisted to stare into her eyes. His intense blue gaze dropped briefly to her mouth, sending a wave of heat washing over her. Then he abruptly jumped to his feet, breaking all contact.

It took her a moment to realize there had been a knock at the door. Brady with DEA agent Doug Bridges.

She rose, smiling at the newcomer. If she were honest with herself, she'd admit that if Reed was any other cop, she probably would have taken his advice about leaving him here in favor of staying with her family.

But he wasn't any other cop. He was the man who'd saved her life. And the guy she'd been interested in getting to know better prior to Ivan Garcia holding her hostage.

No, she was not leaving Reed to stumble through this mess alone. She intended to help in any way possible.

THE TWO-BEDROOM SUITE seemed downright tiny once Rhy, Brady, and Doug Bridges were settled in the living area. Reed did his best to ignore the sizzle of awareness he felt every time Alanna brushed against him.

Why didn't one of her brothers wise up and pull her out of here? She was a nurse, not a cop. Her full name being in the paper was bad, but still, there had to be another way. He was afraid she'd end up getting hurt because of the target on his back. Every time he saw those sutures in her neck, a wave of guilt hit hard.

"I heard about the rival gang shooting." Doug met his gaze. "You were there and so was our task force member, Tate Brown."

"Correct. Me and my rookie partner, Wesley Durango, were the first to arrive, followed shortly afterward by Geoff Watkins and his partner, Kyle Zimmer." Reed watched Bridges's expression for any reaction to the names. "Somehow, Wesley ended up dead and stashed in our squad while it was outside the ED parking lot."

Doug whistled. "You think Tate is involved?"

"I don't know." He quickly explained about the times he'd called the precinct only to have had gunmen show up at his location. "I ditched my phone, and Alanna has turned hers off too. That's why this room was arranged through the DA's office."

"I can give you the little I know about Tate Brown," Doug offered. "He's been on the force for five years, and his record is clean. Nothing to indicate he would have any reason to team up with a gang."

"No rips?" Rhy frowned. "Almost every cop that works hard ends up getting dinged at some point. Sounds as if he's too clean."

Doug arched a brow. "Is there such a thing? Maybe Tate just follows the rules."

"Rhy's right," Reed said. "It's impossible to always follow every rule when you're on the street. There are always scenarios where a cop has to trust his gut or his judgment based on experience that might go against the so-called rules."

"Does that mean you have reprimands in your file?" Doug asked.

"Absolutely." Reed didn't hesitate to tell the truth. "I went against my orders twice in my career and got dinged both times. Despite the fact that the order was a bad one."

"I agree," Rhy chimed in. "There's always going to be times where the rules don't apply exactly as written." When Doug looked like he would protest, Rhy raised a hand. "I'm not talking about cases of excessive force or anything like that. I'm talking about the kind of thing Reed mentioned."

"Okay, whatever." Doug threw up his hands. "Regardless, I don't think there's any reason to believe Tate Brown is dirty."

"I think we should talk to him," Alanna said. "Maybe he will explain what he saw the night Reed's partner was murdered."

Doug looked thoughtful for a moment. "I'll call him. See if he's willing to do that."

"With all due respect, don't make it a request," Reed said. "We need to know what happened that night. Obviously, Garcia was shot and tried to use Alanna as a hostage to escape going back to prison, but my partner's murder is a key component to this."

"I think the bigger issue is the price that the Blood Kings put on your head," Alanna pointed out. She looked at Doug. "Did Tate Brown have any inside information about gang activity? A snitch that may know something relevant?"

Doug nodded slowly. "During our last meeting Tate mentioned a snitch who was giving him information about the Blood Kings. Unfortunately, the information always seemed to be a day late."

Reed's interest spiked. "What do you mean?"

"The snitch apparently told Tate there was a gun deal going down on a specific night. We had cops at the location but found nothing. We discovered the deal went down the previous night."

Warning bells sounded in the back of Reed's mind. "Maybe that's because Tate is involved. He's pretending to help when in reality he's working with the gangs for a piece of the pie."

Doug leveled him with a hard stare. "Or it's the snitch who is working both sides, giving false intel to Officer Brown."

"We know someone within the fifth district is involved." Reed strove to keep his voice even. "That's been proven twice in a matter of hours. No other way to explain how gunmen targeted us so quickly. A snitch wouldn't be able to track my phone to discover my location. But a cop would."

Doug's lips tightened, then he sighed. "Okay, fine. We'll go with your theory. The insider may not be Tate himself, though, it could be his superior. It's not just the lower-level cops that can be corrupted by greed."

"I agree. I'm sure it wasn't easy when your boss was arrested back in July," Rhy said.

"You know firsthand what it feels like to be betrayed by someone you should have been able to trust." Reed caught the tiny nod Doug gave him. "Okay, we won't jump to any conclusions, but we'll still have to operate under the premise that all are guilty until cleared. Let's start by setting up a meeting with Tate Brown."

"Sure." Doug pulled out his phone. "He'll think it's weird if I have him come to a meeting at a hotel, though. Thoughts on where to set this up?"

"The FBI office," Brady said. "I'm sure we can get Reed, Rhy, and Alanna there safely."

"Not me, sorry." Rhy's troubled gaze was on his phone. "Devon has a doctor's appointment, and I'd like to go along."

"What's wrong?" Alanna asked. "Is she having pain? Bleeding? What?"

"A few contractions, which her doctor says can be normal." Rhy stood. "Still, I'd like to be there for her."

"You should go," Reed agreed, keeping his gaze averted from Alanna. If it was his wife, he'd insist on being there too. And where had that thought come from? He hadn't planned on having a family. Not after Olivia had broken things off with him. He should have known better than to get involved with a fellow cop.

"Go, Rhy. We're fine," Brady agreed.

"Thanks." Rhy looked distracted as he headed for the door, but then he paused to meet Reed's gaze. "Keep me in the loop, Carmichael. Especially if there are any more attempts on your life."

What Rhy really wanted to know was if Alanna was in harm's way, which was understandable. He nodded. "I will."

Rhy left, leaving Brady and Doug behind.

"Before we go anywhere, let's make sure Tate is around to meet." Doug scrolled through his phone, likely searching for the cop's contact information. He found it and pressed the button, lifting his hand for silence.

Several seconds passed before Tate answered. Reed watched Doug's features for insight as to what was being said.

"Hey, sorry to bother you," Doug said in a casual tone. "I have a few thoughts about the task force and an idea of where to focus our energy next. Any chance you can meet me at the FBI office?"

More silence as Doug listened. Reed was frustrated that the fed kept his gaze impassive as he listened.

"Sure, eleven o'clock works fine. Thanks. See you then." Doug lowered the phone and glanced at his watch. "We're set to meet in an hour."

"Good." Alanna looked relieved and determined. "I have a feeling this chat will help lead us to another suspect."

Reed still thought Tate himself might be involved but didn't mention it. "Brady, where did you park?"

"In the lot, why?"

"I think it's best if Alanna and I leave through a side exit, rather than using the front doors." He wasn't taking any chances. Not with her life. "I noticed an exit at the end of this hallway. I'd like you drive over there to pick us up."

"That works." Brady stood. "Doug, why don't you head out first and make sure we can use one of the interview rooms."

"Got it." Doug rose and headed for the door, pausing to glance back. "We should talk about how to approach this with Brown before he gets there. I don't want to accuse him of anything we can't prove."

"I know," Brady agreed. "The office is only twenty minutes away. We should have plenty of time to formulate a plan."

After the two federal agents left, he turned to Alanna. "Are you ready?"

"Yes." She wrinkled her nose. "I'm not a fan of sitting around. It feels good to be doing something."

He understood. This wasn't exactly easy for him either. "We'll give Brady a few minutes to get in position."

"I hope Devon is okay." Alanna's expression reflected her concern. "I'm no expert in obstetrics, but I think Braxton Hicks contractions can be as early as four to six weeks prior to a due date. She has seven weeks to go yet." She gnawed her lower lip. "I hope she doesn't have the baby prematurely."

"Rhy will let you know if there's anything to worry about." He smiled reassuringly. "Do they know if they're having a boy or a girl?"

"No, Devon wanted the baby's gender to be a surprise." Alanna smiled. "We tried to get her to do a gender reveal party, but she refused. We had to settle for a regular baby shower."

He'd never been to one, so he didn't have anything to add. When he judged there had been enough time for Brady to get into position, he turned to the door. "Ready?"

Alanna nodded, patting her jeans pocket as if to make

sure she had the room key. He opened the door, looking both ways before stepping into the hall. He took Alanna's hand and led the way to the side exit where Brady was waiting for them.

Once they were settled with Reed up front and Alanna in the back, Brady headed away from the downtown hotel. He glanced over at him. "I know this case is personal to you, but it would be best if you let Doug and I take the lead in this interview."

It chafed, but he nodded. "Okay. But I would recommend you start with the shooting between the Latino Hombres and Blood Kings. See if Tate can shed any light on what went down that evening. We assume a turf war of some kind, but specifics would be helpful."

"Sounds reasonable." Brady concentrated on navigating through traffic for a moment.

"Shouldn't Tate's snitch have known about the incident prior to it going down?" Alanna asked.

"Maybe." Brady lifted a shoulder. "I'd like to get the name of Tate's snitch. I suspect he's not being forthcoming about everything he knows."

"Shocker," Reed muttered. He didn't have much faith in snitches. Sure, they could sometimes give good insight into what might be happening on the street, but they were in it for the money, mostly to feed a drug habit. Trusting an addict wasn't smart. But then again, what else did they have to go on?

A big fat nothing.

"Does Tate Brown work out of your district, Reed?"

He glanced over his shoulder at Alanna. "Yeah, he does. Which is why I still think he may be involved in this." He made a mental note to talk to his buddy Geoff. It was possible Geoff saw something last night that would explain his partner's death.

"If he is, we'll figure it out," Brady assured him.

Their plan of getting to the FBI offices early came to a screeching halt. Dozens of red taillights flashed as traffic on the interstate came to a grinding stop. Reed craned his neck but couldn't see anything beyond the packed cars.

"Accident?" Alanna asked, her brow furrowed with concern.

Reed had no doubt she'd jump out to assist as needed. He glanced over his shoulder. "Could be anything. Lots of construction around here."

The joke in Wisconsin was that there weren't four seasons in Wisconsin, just two. Winter and construction.

For long moments, traffic didn't move. Not even an inch. Reed tried to curb his impatience, but it wasn't easy.

"Relax," Brady teased. "Everyone is likely stuck in the same traffic jam. We won't miss anything."

"Except coming up with an interview plan," Reed pointed out.

Brady nodded and used the dashboard communication to call Doug. "Are you stuck in this mess?"

"What mess?" Doug sounded confused.

"We're in a traffic jam. Probably an accident." Brady inched forward. "We may not be on time."

"Doug, it's Reed," he quickly interjected. "I would like you to consider asking Tate about the night of the shooting. See if he's heard anything from his snitch about what went down."

"I can do that," Doug agreed. "Sounds like Tate might end up in the same traffic jam you're in. I must have missed it."

"Lucky you," Reed said.

Brady moved another few inches. "There's movement up ahead. Hopefully, we'll be out of this, soon."

"I'll be here," Doug said. "Any other thoughts on what we need to ask?"

"The name of his snitch, if he'll give it up." Brady grimaced as they moved a whole foot this time. "I'm curious if the snitch has intel on both the Blood Kings and the Latino Hombres or just one of the gangs."

"He didn't want to give us the name when we initiated the group, but based on the price that's been put on Reed's head, that is now a nonnegotiable point." Doug's voice was somber. "I'm done playing around."

Reed cocked a brow, wondering if Doug was beginning to lean toward Tate being their guy. "Glad to hear it. I don't have anything else to add, do you?" He glanced at Brady.

"I don't think we should tip our hand about our suspicions," Brady said. "If anything seems hinky, we can put a tail on him. That may reveal more."

"I like it." Reed stared through the windshield. If he could have sprouted wings to fly over the traffic jam, he would have.

"The Lord is testing our patience." Alanna sighed. "Especially mine."

"Looks like things are moving," Brady said. "We should be at the FBI offices before Tate. See you there, Doug."

"Later." Doug disconnected from the line.

The traffic did move, but not nearly as quickly as Reed would have liked. He looked forward to interviewing Tate Brown. The cop likely knew something that could help.

The next mile was slow, but soon they passed what appeared to be a dump truck and a mangled car. Alanna craned her neck as if looking for injured passengers, but there was no sign of anyone looking in need of assistance.

The road ahead was clear, so Brady hit the gas to make up for lost time.

Reed had never been to the FBI office building and was a little surprised when Brady pulled into the parking lot of a nondescript brown brick building. The surface parking lot was only about halfway full, and he wondered if there was another parking area for the federal agents themselves.

Brady threw the gearshift into park. "Reed, you'll need to leave your weapon in the car. I'll drive you both back to the hotel. You'll both have to sign in and wear visitor ID tags."

"Understood." Reed took a moment to remove his holster, weapon, and extra clip. He stored everything inside the glove box. "Ready."

As they emerged from the SUV, another car drove up beside them. Reed and Alanna were a few steps ahead, but Reed turned, his hand going to a gun that wasn't there. It took a moment for him to recognize MPD Officer Tate Brown.

"Looks like our guy showed early," he said to Brady.

"Yeah." Brady frowned. "Go ahead, I'll wait for him."

Reed took Alanna's arm to urge her forward when the loud crack of gunfire rang out. He instantly yanked Alanna to the ground, covering her with his body.

"Officer down!" Brady shouted, making Reed realize he was yelling into his phone. "Repeat, officer down!"

Which officer? Reed lifted his head and turned to look behind him. Brady was crouched beside the SUV while the body of Tate Brown was lying facedown on the ground. A pool of blood oozed from beneath the man's face.

Their only lead on finding out who had murdered his rookie partner was dead.

CHAPTER NINE

"What happened?" Alanna pushed against Reed's body. "Who's hit?"

"Your brother is fine." Reed did not budge beneath her attempt to shove him aside. "Stay down. The cop we were planning to interview was shot."

"Officer Brown?" She craned her neck to peer around Reed's body to see for herself. Then she gave him another solid shove. "Let me up! I need to stabilize him until the ambulance gets here."

"There's nothing you can do," Reed said grimly. "He's gone."

"You don't know that," she snapped. With an abrupt twist, a move she'd perfected when wrestling with Aiden, she freed herself from his grip. Rising to a crouch, she ran over to the fallen man.

"Alanna, get down!" Brady shouted. "We haven't spotted the shooter!"

She ducked her head but continued her quick examination of the injured man. When she noticed the entry wound on the back of his head, her heart sank. Still, she moved her fingers around to the front of his neck to check for a pulse.

Nothing.

Reed was right. Tate Brown was dead. Her shoulders sagged in defeat.

"Alanna." Reed came up behind her, covering her back with his body. She turned to look up at him. His fierce expression reflected his annoyance. "Please come back to the SUV."

She reluctantly nodded.

"Brady, cover us." Reed spoke in a loud tone. She could see FBI agents running out of the building in response to the gunfire. Reed rose and pulled her up beside him. "Hurry," he urged. "We need to be far away from here."

"What about the police?" Sirens indicated local cops would be arriving at any moment. "Shouldn't we stay and talk to them?"

"No." Reed's tense tone was firm. He opened the passenger-side door. "Get in."

Glancing through the windshield toward Brady, she sent a questioning look. Her brother nodded, so she scrambled inside. She had to assume Brady would cover for them with the local authorities.

It wasn't until Reed had driven the SUV away from the FBI office building that the implication of this brutal murder struck deep. "He was killed to prevent him from speaking with us."

"Exactly." Reed's jaw was so tight she expected to hear his teeth crack beneath the pressure. "No way was that a coincidence."

"I agree." She shivered, suddenly chilled despite the warm sunlight. She looked at Reed. "Wait a minute, is it possible one of us was the real target? That Officer Brown simply got in the way?"

"Not likely." Reed caught her gaze for a moment before he turned his attention back to the road. "The bullet struck the back of his head with a precision that was lacking in the other shooting attempts. This cold-blooded murder was done by a pro. Not a gang banger looking to add to his street cred, like the guy outside Rosie's Diner."

"Dear Lord Jesus," she whispered, praying for strength. "A cop? You think another cop shot him? Why? What's going on?"

"Whatever it is, it's bigger than we originally thought." Reed shook his head in frustration. "I wish I understood how this is linked to the gang shooting that first night. How could something like that result in two cops being brutally shot and killed?"

Nausea swirled in her belly. Several of her siblings were cops, including Kyleigh. She'd always known they put their lives on the line each day, but she hadn't fully appreciated what they faced until now.

With a shaky hand, she tucked her hair behind her ear. "Where are we going?"

"Back to the City Central Hotel." Reed's gaze moved constantly from the cars on either side of them to the rearview mirror. "As far as I can tell, that was the only place we've been safely under the radar. I imagine the shooter was surprised that we were at the FBI offices when Brown showed up."

"I guess we'll never know what Tate was going to tell us. Especially the name of his snitch." She stared blindly out the window before turning toward Reed. "Do you think he was killed because he was in on it? Or because he was too close to uncovering the truth?"

Reed was silent for a few seconds before answering. "I'm leaning toward the latter. If he was part of this, he could easily have given us false information, sending us down a different path while shielding the truth. The only way taking him down makes sense was if he had suspicions he was about to share."

"Quite a setback."

"Yeah." Reed sighed. "I'm sure your brother will call if he learns anything useful."

"He will." She tried to think positive. Maybe Tate had some information on his cell phone or in the vehicle that would help. "How long does it take to process a crime scene?"

"With the feds involved?" The barest hint of a smile tugged at the corner of Reed's mouth. "Probably all day."

"I'm sure Brady will put a rush on whatever they find." She couldn't help smiling in return. "It's good to have inside connections."

"That's true." Reed's expression turned serious. "I'm impressed with the way your brothers jumped in to help."

"When was the last time you saw your brother?" Traffic moved quickly, without too much of a gaper's block. As they passed, she noted the earlier accident scene had been completely cleared.

"Last year at Christmas." Reed glanced at her. "Eric and I shared the holiday with our grandparents, but it was short and sweet. I had to work the night shift, so we only had time for a Christmas brunch."

She couldn't fathom going ten months without seeing her family. "With our various jobs requiring weekend and holiday shifts, we can't always get off at the same time either. But this year, it looks like our schedules will finally come together so we're all off work on Christmas morning."

"All of you?" Reed cocked a brow. "How in the world did that happen?"

"Rhy would say that God works in mysterious ways. Elly is new in her role as an EMT, and we thought for sure she'd have to work Christmas Day, but she's on duty Christmas Eve instead." She didn't let on about her concern that Elly may not be working as an EMT at all by the Christmas holiday. She often prayed the youngest Finnegan would find her way.

Not that she hadn't tried. Elly entered the police academy but couldn't pass the physical requirements. Then she'd been admitted into the nursing program but had dropped out of that after two years of study.

They all hoped Elly would settle down sooner than later.

"Sounds like it will be crowded at the homestead, especially since so many of your siblings are married."

Reed's comment snapped her back to the present. "That's true. But I'm thrilled for my older brothers and sister. They deserve to be happy."

He nodded, then exited the freeway. She noticed he took several turns as he headed toward the City Central Hotel. She turned to look behind them but didn't see anything suspicious.

Not that spotting a tail was her area of expertise. "Anyone following us?"

"No." He frowned. "Although I would feel better if Brady and Doug found the shooter."

She wholeheartedly agreed that arresting the shooter would take some of the pressure off. And would hopefully shed light on who was responsible.

Reed took more side streets, going as far down as the lakefront before turning to head toward the hotel. When they arrived, he parked in the farthest corner of the lot, as far from the main entrance as possible.

"We'll use the side door we came out of earlier." He tucked his hand beneath her elbow, steering her in that direction.

Her pulse didn't settle down until they were inside the suite with the door locked. She dropped onto the sofa, putting a hand over her thundering heart. "I'm not cut out for this."

"I'm sorry." Reed appeared upset at her comment, making her wince.

"It's fine. Ignore my whining."

He surprised her by cradling her hand between his. "Putting you in danger bothers me. I don't want you anywhere in the line of fire. Will you please reconsider staying with one of your siblings?"

"I would if I could." She was tired of this tune he kept singing. "Brady has a wife and a six-year-old son. You know Devon is pregnant, and I'm convinced Joy is too. If there was a viable option, I'd take it. Please stop pressing me on this." Her fault for voicing her fear. "Let's just focus on our next steps. Whatever they are."

He stared at her for a long moment before looking away. "Okay, but if you decide at some point you want out, tell me."

"I promise." She frowned. "I'm hungry. Should we walk over to the café to grab a bite to eat?"

"No. Here's the room service menu." He stood to grab the booklet off the desk. "Order whatever you like. It's on the DA's office, remember?"

That made her smile. "Okay."

Reed paced the room as she reviewed the limited offerings. Normally she had a salad for lunch, but there was no telling when or if they'd get dinner, so she chose something more substantial. She handed the menu back. "I'll have the club wrap."

"Great." Reed crossed to the phone to place their order.

Insane to think about how much had happened in such a few short hours. Yet they were still no closer to uncovering the truth.

At this rate, she feared they never would.

THOSE MOMENTS outside the FBI office replayed over and over in Reed's mind until he thought he might go crazy. He'd never anticipated Tate Brown would be brutally shot and murdered in front of a federal building.

Suddenly he straightened. Cameras! There were cameras mounted around each of the precincts scattered around the city, the feds must have their office wired for sight and sound too. Probably more so than the local cop shops.

He turned to face Alanna. "I'm calling your brother for an update."

"Go ahead, but weren't you the one who told me it would take a while for them to process the scene?" Her gaze was skeptical. "Doubt they know much of anything at this point."

"I hadn't considered the cameras." He pulled out his disposable phone to call her brother, but another phone rang, catching his attention. Glancing at Alanna, he saw her concerned expression.

"Hold on, this is Rhy." She lifted the device to her ear. "Rhy? How's Devon? Is the baby okay?"

He moved closer to support her in case her brother was

calling with bad news. Her brow furrowed as she listened, then she met his gaze. "Okay, thanks for letting me know. Do you think Elly will be all right at the homestead alone?"

"What's going on?" He couldn't help feeling vested in Rhy and Devon's situation.

"Okay, it's good that Colin and Faye will be there too. I don't think any of our family members should be alone at this time."

Reed felt certain there was something going on with Devon and the baby.

"Okay, Rhy. Give Devon a hug and kiss for me. And please let me know if her situation changes, okay?"

"What situation?" Reed asked.

Alanna sighed as she pocketed the phone. "The doctor has admitted Devon for observation. She's having contractions, but they're not regular. Her doctor wants her on bedrest for a while."

"How much longer does she have to go?" He couldn't imagine how a woman could be on bedrest for several months.

"Seven weeks." Alanna's expression was full of concern. "Rhy mentioned the doctor was confident that even if she delivered early, the baby would be okay."

He didn't know anything about having premature babies. "I guess that's good to hear."

"We had a woman come into the ED in labor when she was six weeks early. The baby was delivered at four pounds six ounces." She tried to smile. "The good news was that the baby's lungs worked great. She cried loudly and didn't need to be on a ventilator."

The image of a tiny baby being on a ventilator made his stomach knot with tension. "How is Rhy doing? Is he holding up?"

"He's being strong for Devon's sake." Alanna tucked her hair behind her ear. "But I can tell he's worried. He'll never say that to any of us, always wanting to come across as the strong father figure, but he's troubled over Devon's need to stay in the hospital."

"Hey, any soon-to-be-father would be the same way." He offered a reassuring smile. "You're a nurse, you know that Devon and her baby will be fine."

"Yeah. As long as nothing else goes wrong." She shook her head. "The tough part about being in the medical field is imagining the worst-case scenario."

"Maybe try leaning on your faith."

Her eyes widened, and she smiled, a real smile that reached her eyes. "You're right, Reed. I will pray for Devon, her baby, and Rhy."

"I will too." He hesitated, then added, "Although I haven't been to church in years."

"That's okay. God doesn't mind." Her smile widened. "He's always there, waiting for you to come back to Him."

Was she right about that? He wasn't entirely convinced. He turned away, belatedly remembering his intent to call her brother. He placed the call. The other end of the line rang four times before Brady answered.

"Is something wrong?" Brady asked.

"No, we're fine," Reed assured him. "But I'm wondering if your cameras caught a glimpse of the shooter. He may be someone I recognize from the initial scene of the gang shooting."

"We're pouring through the video now," Brady said. "We identified a black SUV that pulled into the lot five seconds after Tate did. Looks like he was followed to the FBI office."

That wasn't reassuring. "I'd think he'd be on alert for a tail."

"Yeah, well, who knows?" Brady sighed. "The shooter stayed in the car, so we didn't get a clear view of his face."

A bull's-eye shot made from the front seat of a car? The thought lifted the hairs on the back of his neck. "The shooter has to be another cop."

"That's our working theory," Brady agreed. "I can send you the pictures we have, but I don't have high hopes you'll be able to identify him. The sun glinted off the windshield interfering with the ability to see the guy's face clearly. We have techs working to sharpen the image, but I don't have the improved version yet."

"Send me what you have, along with any better pictures your techs are able to create," Reed said. "What about Tate's phone and his car? Find anything interesting there?"

"The crime scene techs are processing the car for prints. We're hoping the snitch was in the vehicle at some point and that he's in the system. There are several calls on Tate's phone. It's going to take us some time to find out who the numbers belong to."

He frowned. "I'm sure the snitch used a burner phone."

"Agreed. But if we can get the snitch's prints, we'll be able to track him down regardless of the phone number he's been using."

Feds could often be territorial, unwilling to share their information with local authorities. Brady seemed to be the exact opposite, and a wave of admiration for Alanna's brother washed over him. "Thanks for the update, I appreciate everything you're doing. I wish I could be there to help track down leads."

"I'd rather you stay focused on protecting Alanna,"

Brady said. "I nearly had a heart attack when she rushed over to tend to Tate."

"You and me both." He was not happy at how she'd managed to wiggle away. She flashed him a knowing look as if she knew they were talking about her. "I tried to tell her that he was already dead, but she wouldn't listen. I guess she needed to see for herself."

"Sounds like Alanna." Brady chuckled. "She's stubborn."

Wasn't that a trait all the Finnegans shared? He'd only met a handful of them, but yeah, he was pretty sure it was. "Will you continue to update us on your progress?"

"Yes." Brady's voice turned solemn. "We've never had a shooting outside the bureau, especially not a cop. Donovan, our special agent in charge, is pretty upset and is demanding I work the case with Doug."

"Okay." Reed knew there wasn't anything else he could do from the hotel. "Don't forget to send me the photo of the shooter." Remembering he didn't have a smart phone, he added, "Use my email, okay?" He quickly gave him the email address.

"Sending the pictures now. Later, Reed." Brady ended the call.

"I suppose Brady is mad at me too."

"He's not." Reed cast her a sideways glance as he turned on the laptop. "He called you stubborn."

"Like he should talk," she groused.

Reed had a response from his email to his former partner, Nate Jackson, but left it unopened in favor of looking at the email from Brady. When it popped into his box, he noticed it was from Brady's private email, not his official one within the bureau. Did that mean he was helping Reed without his boss's approval? He found himself hoping the fed didn't get himself in hot water over this.

When he opened the attachments, he inwardly groaned at the blurry images that bloomed on the screen.

"What did Brady send you?" Alanna leaned over his shoulder to see the computer screen and the two photographs he'd pulled up so they were side by side. "Really? That's the best they could do?"

"They have a tech working on sharpening the image." He stared at the pictures, trying to place the blurred features with a cop from his precinct.

It was no use. He shook his head, swallowing his frustration. "I can't place this guy as a fellow cop or anyone else that I know."

"Me either." She straightened, giving him some breathing room. Why was she so close? Her flowery-scented shampoo was messing with his head.

"I, uh, expect the food will be here soon." He tried to edge past her.

"Reed." She stopped him with a hand on his arm. Oddly, he could feel the warmth of her fingers radiating through his long sleeve.

"What?" He swallowed hard at the way her brown eyes searched his.

"I appreciate everything you're doing for me." Her smile brightened her face. "Not just keeping me safe, but you've been really sweet in showing concern for my family."

He stared at her, having no clue how to respond. He didn't want to admit how much he'd come to care about her siblings. It seemed as if they'd been working together forever rather than less than twenty-four hours. "Anyone else would do the same," he finally said.

"No, they wouldn't." She stepped closer. Alarm bells

jangled in his mind. "You're special, Reed. I hope you know that."

"I'm not special, I'm just a street cop." Why wasn't the food here yet? He cleared his throat. "Not to mention I'm also the guy who put you in danger."

"Pretty sure the Blood Kings did that when Garcia took me hostage, forcing you to shoot him. I owe you so much." She lifted up onto her tiptoes to brush a kiss across his mouth. In the back of his mind, he understood she only meant to thank him, but the brief kiss instantly morphed into something more.

His arms betrayed him by circling her waist and drawing her close. He angled his mouth over hers, kissing her the way he'd wanted to for months now. Not just the past few hours, but way back to their first meeting early in the summer. The day he'd brought a patient in his custody to the ED for medical care.

Alanna kissed him back, sending wave after wave of sizzling heat washing over him. He pulled her even closer still until some strange sound intruded.

She broke off their kiss, leaning back to laugh up at him. "I think our food's here."

What food? Oh yeah. Their room service lunch.

He managed to pull himself together long enough to look through the peephole. A man stood there with a tray of food.

See, this was why kissing Alanna was a bad idea. What if a gunman had shown up instead?

Getting emotionally involved with Alanna wasn't smart. He needed to keep his head screwed on straight.

Before the Blood Kings took advantage of his weakness.

CHAPTER TEN

The bemused expression in Reed's eyes made her smile. He was so handsome, even if he was more stubborn than anyone in her entire family. Kissing him had been better than she'd imagined, but reality was beginning to sink in. She knew any sort of relationship between them was ill-timed. They had bigger things to worry about. It would have been much better if they'd had a chance to get to know each other under normal circumstances.

Instead of being thrust together by danger.

Reed was determined to protect her, which meant she needed to take their situation at face value. Reed might care about her, but that didn't mean he wanted more.

She'd kissed him, not the other way around.

He brought in the food tray and set it on the small table near the kitchenette.

"Smells good." She'd ordered a wrap with fries. She'd go back to the gym once this was over. For now, after being barraged by gunfire, she decided to live in the moment. And that included eating French fries.

He removed the metal covers, setting them aside.

Once they were seated, she reached for his hand. He looked surprised, then bowed his head when he realized she wanted to say grace. "Dear Lord Jesus, we thank You for protecting us today. Please continue guiding us on Your path to seeking those who wish us harm. Amen."

"And please keep all the Finnegans safe in Your care." Reed's voice was low and husky. "Amen."

"That was nice of you to include my family." Her smile faded as she remembered Rhy and Devon. "I'd like to check in with Rhy later to see how Devon is doing."

"Of course." He picked up his BLT sandwich and took a bite. He looked lost in thought, no doubt about the case.

Sobering to know their only lead had been murdered right in front of their eyes. Were all the members of the joint task force at risk? The thought made her shiver.

"Are you cold?" Reed's keen blue gaze didn't miss a thing.

"No, just thinking about the task force." She picked up a fry. "I'm worried that other members are at risk."

"I had the same thought." Reed scowled at his sandwich. "That only makes me more convinced that a cop is involved. Someone on the inside who knows about the task force and possibly the name of the snitch."

Selfishly, she was secretly relieved her brothers weren't involved in the task force. But then she understood that it didn't matter. Tarin, Rhy, and Brady had inserted themselves into the case. They were as involved now as anyone else. Maybe more so.

Her previous hunger faded at the dark thoughts. She caught Reed's gaze. "What can we do while we're waiting? I don't want to sit around doing nothing."

"Me either. We have the computer, maybe there's something to be learned by looking into Tate Brown's social media posts. Oh, and I have an email from my former partner. Maybe he has some insight."

"Social media?" She nibbled on another fry. "My cop siblings aren't on any social media sites. Working a task force on gang violence, you'd think Tate would stay off too."

"That's true." Reed's expression turned thoughtful. "But maybe that theory doesn't hold true for gang members."

"Why on earth would gang members be on social media?" She couldn't imagine it.

"For one thing, these kids grew up in a world that used social media more so than we did. For them, it's natural. Not to mention, it's a way to communicate with others. I'm sure they're using privacy settings, but if we find something interesting, maybe Brady can help us cut through red tape to get access into their accounts."

"If Brady can, he will." The idea of having something productive to do helped spark her appetite.

"I know." Reed grinned. "He's not like most feds who are stingy with intel."

She tipped her head to the side. "Have you worked with federal agents often?"

"Just one big case two years ago." All mirth faded from his features. "There was a prostitution ring involving teenage sex-trafficked victims that we raided. I don't think your brother was a part of that."

"Working in the emergency department, we're always on alert for possible victims of sex trafficking." She sighed. "It's a struggle because they're so afraid that they rarely cooperate."

"I know." He waved a hand. "Let's not focus on all the depressing criminal activity that goes on in a city our size. We need to concentrate on the Blood Kings."

"Okay." She did her best to shake off the sense of help-lessness. Every day she went to work she was determined to take good care of her patients. But some days were more difficult than others.

They ate in silence for several moments. Her thoughts kept going back to her patient. "Did you notice Ivan Garcia's teardrop tattoos?"

"Yeah." He eyed her over the rim of his water bottle. "The Latino Hombres use them too. I think that practice has carried over from the gangs in Chicago."

"Garcia told me he wasn't going back to jail." Pushing away her empty plate, she propped her elbows on the table and laced her hands together. "He was twenty-three years old and had three teardrop tattoos colored with red ink. I assume those were three people he murdered, but there's no way he could have been released from jail for murder after only a year or so, right? I wonder why he was arrested?"

"We can look that up." Reed finished the last of his fries, then stood to lift their empty tray. He set it outside their room, then reached for the computer. He set it on the table. She inched her chair closer so she could see the screen.

"I forgot about the Wisconsin case search," she murmured as he brought the website up.

"Do you use it to check on your patients?" He looked surprised.

She laughed. "No, only potential dates." She tapped the screen. "Marriages and divorces are listed in here too. This is how I found out the guy I was dating wasn't divorced the way he'd claimed. So much for a doctor being honorable."

"That's true." He sent her a curious look. "I'm sorry about the idiot who lied to you. I'm sure your brothers taught you to research all potential boyfriends."

"They did." It had been incredibly annoying at the time,

but she appreciated their protectiveness now that she was older. "When I was in high school, the guy who asked me to prom had an underage drinking ticket. Rhy hit the roof and refused to let me go."

"I'm sure your date wasn't the only kid in school with an underage drinking ticket," Reed said.

"He was with a group of basketball players who had been caught at a local party. Aiden came to my defense, and in the end, Rhy let me go as long as we double-dated with Aiden and his girlfriend." She smiled at the memory. "Justin wasn't thrilled, but he was a perfect gentleman. Mostly because Rhy sat in the living room cleaning his service weapon when he picked me up."

Reed chuckled. "I can picture that so very clearly."

"Right? It's no wonder Justin disappeared from my life shortly afterward."

"Any decent guy would respect your family." He arched a brow. "If having a cop as an older brother scared him off, he wasn't worth your time."

"Funny, that's what Aiden said too." She shrugged. "That next week, I discovered I'd been accepted into the nursing program at the University of Wisconsin in Milwaukee as a direct entry student. They didn't offer those positions to everyone, so that was a really big deal. I decided Justin wasn't part of my future. His loss, not mine."

"Smart girl." Reed grinned. "I couldn't agree more."

She felt herself flush and decided it was time to change the subject. "Let's see what we can find out about Ivan Garcia. Oh, and I need to call Rhy too."

Reed turned his attention back to the computer while she made the call.

"Are you okay?" Rhy asked in lieu of a greeting.

"Yes, I'm calling to check on Devon and the baby."

"Oh, she's fine. The contractions are still irregular and not very strong, according to the staff here. And they gave her fluids, thinking she was dehydrated." Rhy hesitated, then asked, "Are you and Reed okay? Do you need anything? I hate that I had to leave you there without more support."

"We're fine, Rhy. Perfectly safe." She decided this wasn't the time to fill him in on the shooting outside the FBI building. Better for him to hear that news from Brady. "Do you think they're going to keep Devon overnight?"

"It looks that way. But if her condition is unchanged by morning, they'll allow her to go home on bedrest."

Bedrest? She winced. "Guess it's a good thing you saved up all your personal days after all, huh?"

"Yeah. Listen, the doctor is making rounds, so I need to run. Take care."

"We will. You do the same." She disconnected from the call, feeling better about Devon's condition, even if she'd need to stay on bedrest for a while.

She turned her attention to Reed who was working on the computer. "Everything okay?" he asked without looking away from the screen.

"Yes. Devon and the baby are stable. Did you get into the case site?"

"Yep. Looks like Ivan Garcia was charged for reckless endangerment while operating a motor vehicle and for illegal possession of a firearm." Reed grimaced. "He only did eighteen months before being placed on probation."

"Eighteen months?" She shook her head. "Doesn't seem right."

"I know. It's frustrating." He searched for a bit longer, then opened a popular social media account.

She leaned forward to get a better look. "How can you see anything if you're not on there?"

"I have a page, but it doesn't have any personal information about me, and it's under my middle name." He tapped the screen. "Paul R. Carr is really me."

"And you have a cartoon profile picture too." She glanced over at him. "I'm surprised this hasn't been flagged as a fake account."

"There are hundreds of thousands of fake accounts." Reed waved off her concern. "Mine is more innocuous than most. Let's see if we can locate Ivan Garcia."

He poked around a bit. "I think I may have found him." He turned the laptop so she could see it better. "What do you think? Is this our guy?"

"Yes, that's him." She knew Ivan's face would be imprinted on her memory forever. Then she leaned forward. "Hey, in this picture he only has two red teardrops inked on his face, not three."

Reed turned the computer to see the discrepancy for himself. "That's interesting. The tattoo on his face didn't look fresh or new."

She agreed with his assessment. "It also means he killed someone between the time this picture was taken and the time he was brought to the hospital." A chill snaked down her spine.

"There was another guy arrested that same day," Reed said. He clicked through several screens to get back to the circuit court database. "Looks like Javier Patron is a known associate of Garcia. Let's see if we can find his mug shot or if he's on social media too."

"Maybe he was one of the guys who came through the ambulance bay doors to help Ivan escape?"

"It's possible." Reed shook his head. "Unfortunately, I

didn't get a good look at them. I was focused on taking out Garcia."

The image of a young man's face bloomed on the screen when Reed went back to the social media platform where he'd found Garcia. "Is that him?"

"Yeah." Reed tapped the screen. "See that?"

She peered closer to see Javier's face. "It looks like a teardrop that has been colored in blue rather than red."

"Yeah." Reed's expression turned grim. "Blue means he killed a cop."

A cop? She stared in horror at the kid's blank eyes and the small blue teardrop inked on his face.

It was far too easy to imagine another blue teardrop being added to a gang member's face after killing his partner.

And yet another if one of them managed to shoot and kill Reed.

REED HAD HEARD of the blue teardrop as a way of bragging over killing a cop but had never seen one until now.

In his mind, the blue teardrop should be enough for an arrest. But he doubted that fact alone would stick in court. Even though it was well known what the blue teardrop stood for, it wasn't evidence that could be linked to a specific crime.

"That's awful," Alanna murmured.

"Hopefully, there aren't too many blue teardrop tattoos out there." Reed clicked on a few pages, trying to get more access, then sat back with a frown. "He has all privacy settings in place, so I can't see anything but his profile picture."

"We can try Brady, see if he's learned anything." Alanna's expression revealed her concern. He wished he hadn't pointed out what the blue teardrop meant.

"Yeah." He'd hoped to find something useful, but so far, he was coming up empty. "Let's try a few more things first." He went back to the keyboard to see if Wesley Durango had a social media site.

When he saw the rookie's familiar features come up on the screen, he tried not to wince. The kid had not only created a social media page, but he hadn't bothered to use the privacy settings.

"Is that your former partner? Wesley Durango?" Alanna asked.

"Yeah." He glanced at her. "Does he look familiar? Have you seen him in the ED on other occasions?"

She shook her head. "Not that I can remember. He looks so young, Reed. Like barely old enough to shave."

"He was twenty-two." It was always troubling to lose a partner, especially such a young man. "I feel like I failed him in some way."

"It's not your fault." She rested her hand on his arm. "I know it's not easy, but all we can do is keep trying to understand what happened that night. And identify those involved."

She was right, so he focused on the social media page. "Looks like Wesley has friends on here from high school, maybe because most of his fellow officers weren't on social medial."

"You don't think his having a page played a role in his murder?" Alanna looked skeptical. "I hardly think the Blood Kings search for victims on social media."

"No, I believe Wesley either he saw something he shouldn't have, or he was in the way." Reed had trouble looking away from the rookie's young features. Every cop on the job knew the risks, but it wasn't every day that cops were executed with a single bullet to the head.

"No other friends that might be helpful?"

Alanna's question broke into his thoughts. "Not that I can see." He was about to close the screen, then caught sight of a picture of Wes standing near a woman. "Wait a minute." He zoomed in to get a better look.

"What is it?" Alanna was far too astute.

"The woman with him is a cop." He gestured to the screen. "Her name is Olivia Baker, and we dated for about four months."

She frowned. "And you think that's significant in some way?"

"I don't know." He couldn't say why the picture bothered him. "She's free to date whoever she wants, but I still think it's strange."

"Rhy always says to trust your instincts."

"Good advice." His instincts were screaming at him. Olivia hadn't seemed like the type to date a rookie. After they broke up, she started seeing a detective from another precinct. So why the picture with Wesley? His partner was handsome enough, so maybe his lack of rank didn't matter.

His disposable phone rang. He picked it up and answered hesitantly. "Hello?"

"Reed? It's Brady."

"Do you have something for us?" The questioning look on Alanna's features had him putting the call on speaker. "Alanna is here with me."

"Good. I'm glad you're both still safe at the hotel."

Brady's voice faded out as if he were on the move. "I wanted you to know I'm working on a safe house for you."

"That's fine, but we're safe enough here." Reed tried not to show his impatience. "I'm more interested in what evidence you've uncovered so far in the shooting death of Tate Brown. You mentioned checking his vehicle for prints and digging into his cell phone."

"We lifted several prints, and I have Doug Bridges putting them through the federal database now." Brady paused, then added, "The main reason I called was to let you know that the price on your head has doubled."

"Great, so now it's ten grand to kill a cop." The blue teardrop flashed in his mind. "I appreciate the information, but we need the name of Tate Brown's snitch. Without something more to go on, we're dead in the water."

"I know. I'm not happy about the delay either," Brady admitted. "But we want to get this right."

"I understand." He tried to remain patient.

Alanna pointed at the computer screen to prod his memory.

"By the way, we need your help too. We found Ivan Garcia's social media page, but the privacy settings are engaged. Since he's dead, and privacy shouldn't be an issue, we were thinking there might be a way to unlock the profile so we can dig in to see who Garcia's friends and acquaintances are. It's likely one or more of them will be looking to collect that ten-grand reward by coming after me. That's a credible threat that shouldn't be ignored."

"Good idea. Bridges might be able to help with that as part of the task force. He has more involvement and pull there than I do." Brady sounded excited about the information. "I'll get back to you with hopefully the name of Tate's snitch and the info from Garcia's page."

"Thanks." He glanced at Alanna who shrugged. "That's all we need for now."

"Look, Reed, I'm worried about the price on your head." Brady's tone was quiet and serious. "I'd like you to consider using the safe house once I'm given the go-ahead to finalize the arrangements."

"Yeah, okay." It went against the grain, but after seeing Javier Patron's blue teardrop, he knew it would be safer for Alanna to go along with Brady's plan. "Whatever you think is best. Although like I said, we've been safe here."

"Okay, I'll be in touch after I talk to Bridges."

"Thanks." He pushed the end button, disconnecting the call. "I guess there's nothing more we can do but wait."

Turning to the screen, he clicked back on his email from Nate. His buddy's response was full of concern for Reed's welfare. Nate had ended the message with a plea for Reed to call him. Was it safe enough to do that? He wanted to hear what Nate knew, if anything.

"You made a list of the officers from the scene, right?" Alanna's question interrupted his thoughts. "Tate Brown was on the list, but someone killed him. Likely someone who was at the scene that night."

She had a point. He pulled the list from his pocket and set it next to the computer. "It can't hurt to look for social media sites for these guys. Although this one here"—he pointed to Geoff Watkins's name—"is a friend of mine. I know for a fact he doesn't have a page."

"If he's your friend, he's likely not involved. But the others need to be looked at more closely. Is it possible to get their personnel files from the police department?" Alanna asked.

"I can't, but the feds might be able to." He wasn't sure even the federal government had that level of power, but it was another avenue to pursue. "I'll dig into those same officers first to see if we can find anything suspicious."

"Okay." She frowned. "It's frustrating not to have all the information we need to figure out who the dirty cop is."

"Just because I suspect there's someone on the force involved doesn't mean anyone else does."

"They should." She sat up straighter. "Don't the feds get involved in officer-involved shootings?"

"Sometimes, but not always. More often in high-profile cases." He entered one name from the list and had to go through many of the similar names to make sure none of them were a match to the cop he'd worked with that night.

"You can't get more high profile than this one." Alanna reached for a blank slip of paper. "I'm making a list of things to run past Brady. A possible dirty cop inside the precinct would surely warrant a federal investigation."

"Maybe, but everyone is strapped for resources, so don't get your hopes up too high." He was about to narrow the social media search to Milwaukee when he came across a familiar face. "Hey, one of these guys is on here."

"Which one?"

"This one, Doyle Ford." He opened the social media account. "Looks like this hasn't been updated in a while; it states he lives in Steven's Point, Wisconsin." The tiny hairs on the back of his neck lifted. "The female officer we saw standing beside my rookie partner is Olivia Baker. She also transferred to Milwaukee from Steven's Point."

"Point is roughly three hours from here." Alanna stared at him. "You think Olivia and Doyle knew each other before?"

"They must have. That police department isn't nearly as large as Milwaukee." The weird coincidences bothered him. First Olivia standing with Wesley, now this? He didn't like it.

"Isn't it rare for officers to transfer from one city to the next?" Alanna frowned. "I'd think most cops would want a smaller, safer town to work in."

He sat back in the chair. "I asked Olivia that when we were dating. She claimed she wanted to work in a bigger city to help combat crime." At the time he'd admired her dedication. "To answer your question, it's not common for cops to transfer between cities, unless there's a reason like getting married or a spouse that has to relocate."

She nodded thoughtfully. "Why did you and Olivia break up?"

The personal question surprised him. "She wasn't interested in settling down. She left me, not the other way around."

"I'm sorry." Alanna lightly touched his hand.

"It's fine." He stared at her hand for a moment, then turned his attention back to the screen. "I'm going to dig deeper."

He clicked around, feeling a bit like a voyeur even though the page hadn't been updated recently. Then a familiar face caught his attention. "He's friends with another cop, guy by the name of David Branch. Now that I think about it, he was at the scene of the shooting too."

"Another name for the list." Alanna jotted it down.

"That's it, there aren't any other police officers on his list of friends that I can see." He'd half hoped to find Olivia there, but if she'd ever had a social media account, there was no sign of it now. Then a thought struck him. "Wait a minute. The last post from Doyle is from three years ago. If David Branch is a friend, I wonder if he also moved in from the Steven's Point police department?"

"Maybe, but does that matter?"

"I don't know." He wondered again if he was making a big deal out of nothing. Three cops coming from Steven's Point might be unusual, but likely not a precursor to a crime. "We'll gather what information we can and hand it all off to Brady."

As if on cue, his phone rang. This time, he recognized Brady's number. He pressed the speaker button, then connected the call. "It's Reed and Alanna. Please tell us you have good news."

"I have information, not sure it's good or bad," Brady said. "We lifted a set of prints from inside Tate Brown's car belonging to a Javier Patron, a known gang member of the Blood Kings. We can't say for sure he's the snitch, but that's the working theory at the moment."

His gaze clashed with Alanna's as his pulse spiked. "Javier Patron was arrested the same time Ivan Garcia was roughly three years ago. If he's the snitch, I have no doubt he was working against the task force, purposefully giving bad intel to send them down the wrong path. Even worse, he has a blue teardrop tattoo, indicating he's killed a cop."

"We agree with your assessment," Brady said, his tone grave. "The bigger news is that Bridges was able to get into Garcia's social media page. Believe it or not, it appears this guy was doing some gang business using the messenger app. And he was in several conversations with other gang members, including Javier Patron. We're making a list of them now."

Reed sat back in his seat, his mind whirling. "Can we arrest any of them based on what you found?"

"It's possible, especially Javier Patron, but we don't want to pull the trigger on that until we know a lot more about what criminal activities they're involved in." Brady sounded apologetic. "I know that's not what you want to hear, but if we only grab one or two of these guys, the rest will crawl deep into hiding like the cockroaches they are. More importantly, we need to make sure the charges that are filed against them will stick."

Reed knew Brady was right. Still, it burned to know how many other cops would be injured or worse until this gang was taken down and thrown behind bars.

CHAPTER ELEVEN

The news about Javier Patron was disturbing. Alanna leaned forward to speak into the phone. "Brady, why would any cop on the task force trust Javier to provide information while knowing he likely killed a police officer?" Alanna swallowed a wave of frustration. "It doesn't make any sense."

"I wish I had answers for you, sis." Brady sounded as frustrated as she felt. "The whole setup reeks worse than dead fish floating in Lake Michigan."

"Would Bridges be able to give us names of the upper brass who agreed to the task force in the first place?" Reed asked. "It could be one of them is our dirty cop."

"I'll ask Doug to dig into the origin of the task force, but keep in mind, his boss asked him to participate. It would make sense that the police chief was the one to reach out to the feds. I'm not sure his boss knows who's involved from the MPD side of things."

Alanna tried not to show her impatience with the bureaucracy.

"Obviously, this is critical information." She kept her

voice even with an effort. "Who else could have known Tate Brown was coming to a meeting at the FBI headquarters?"

"Trust me, our special agent in charge is not happy about the shooting either. I've convinced him not to storm to city hall, demanding answers, but he does have a phone meeting with the chief in fifteen minutes. If I learn anything new, I'll let you know."

"Okay, thanks, Brady." She gave Reed a questioning look in case he had anything to add.

"My boss is Lieutenant Harvey," Reed said. "He's the phone call I made from Timberland Falls prior to the shooter showing up. The timing seems to indicate either Harvey or Captain Jake Adams is involved. I'd hate to think anyone higher than a captain is dirty. Sergeant Noah Sinclair is a good guy. I trust him more than any of the others."

"I've taken note of the names, along with Charles Simmons, the night-shift cop you spoke to. I agree Noah isn't likely involved. I have to go, but I promise I'll keep you both updated." Brady sounded rushed.

"Thanks." She reached over to disconnect from the call, then let out a sigh. "I was hoping we'd have more by now."

"Me too." Reed's brow furrowed. "Maybe the special agent in charge should storm city hall. A good shake-up could go a long way."

She frowned. "Unless the dirty cop realizes we're onto him and covers his tracks."

Reed looked discouraged as he turned toward the computer. "It's a long shot, but I'll see if either Harvey or Adams are on social media."

She wished there was something she could do to cheer him up. It couldn't be easy to discover the price on your head had doubled in less than twenty-four hours. Or to suspect those you work with to be dirty.

"Any chance you know the names of their wives or kids?" She shifted her chair to see the screen better. "It's more likely they're on one of the platforms."

"Good idea. I know Harvey's wife is Louise." He typed Louise Harvey into the search engine. Surprisingly, several possible matches popped up. Reed seemed to know who he was looking for, though, because he made short work of the list. "Here she is. Louise Margaret Harvey." He turned to catch her eye. "Her site isn't private, which is rather irresponsible of a cop's wife."

"She probably doesn't think it's a big deal since her husband isn't on the site."

Reed shot her a glance. "But you're not on social media because your brothers have drilled safety into you."

"True. And I would never risk anything happening to them even if I wanted to be active there. But honestly, none of us were big into social media anyway." She grinned. "With eight siblings, one of them a twin, there was no reason to go looking for more friends. We had more than enough people tramping through the homestead at any given time."

Reed managed a crooked smile. "I can hardly imagine growing up the way you did."

"There were challenges, but we muddled through." Alanna often wondered if they'd still be this close if their parents had survived. Not that she didn't miss them, because she did. Very much. Yet there was no denying how their family had pulled together in the aftermath of that keen loss, creating a shared closeness that probably wouldn't have been there under different circumstances. As one of the three youngest, they often talked about how much Rhy and Tarin had given up for them.

"There's nothing interesting here. Louise has several friends on her page, but all they talk about are book clubs and lunch dates." Reed dropped his head back to stare at the ceiling. "What are we missing?"

"Fresh air and sunshine?" Normally, she wasn't claustrophobic, but somehow, knowing she had to stay inside only made it more appealing to head out. "Fall is my favorite season, and it's a beautiful day."

He frowned, taking her suggestion to heart. "We've been safe here, so I'd rather not head outside."

She hid her disappointment. "Okay, no problem. We'll keep plugging along."

"Hey." He caught her hand in his. "My only goal is to keep you safe."

"I know." She stared at their joined hands for a moment, remembering their brief but heated kiss. She cared about Reed and refused to leave him alone to deal with this mess he was in. He'd saved her life, the least she could do was to help him now. "It sounds like Brady is working on a safe house anyway, so we won't be here at the hotel for much longer."

"True." Reed squeezed her hand, then released it. "I still feel like we're missing something."

She had no idea how to help him. "Do you think there's any reason to believe the cops who transferred here from Steven's Point are involved?"

"As far as I know there's no gang activity in the smaller cities across the state, they're too far from the city. Every Milwaukee gang has ties to Chicago." He abruptly straightened. "Maybe we should be looking at those officers who transferred from there?"

"Okay, how can we do that?" She frowned. "I'm sure you don't have access to their personnel records."

"No, I don't." He pulled the laptop closer and typed in the name of Charles Simmons.

"Who is that?" She frowned as she looked over his shoulder. "Oh yeah, he's the night-shift cop in your precinct."

"Yes, Simmons called to let me know about the price on my head. His wife is Jolene Simmons." He continued working the keyboard, then sat back in his seat. "Here's a Chicago connection. Jolene mentions on her social media page that she used to teach in the Chicago public school district."

"Okay, but it seems a stretch to assume that just because Charles and Jolene Simmons came to Milwaukee from Chicago that he's in cahoots with the gang."

"Cahoots?" He grinned. "Cute."

"You know what I mean." Her cheeks flushed with embarrassment at being caught using phrases from the TV crime shows she sometimes binge-watched. "Why would he have anything to do with gangs? After all, he didn't have to tell you about the money the Blood Kings were offering as a reward to have you killed. If he was involved, wouldn't he have just kept his mouth shut? Let you find out the hard way?"

"Maybe." Reed sighed. "I don't know what to think. Wesley Durango was the first murder, followed closely by Tate Brown. Two other cops who were on the scene of the original shooting, Doyle Ford and David Branch both transferred from Steven's Point. And Wesley was close to Olivia Baker who also transferred from Steven's Point."

She rested her hand on his arm. "Let's not grasp at

straws. None of what you've uncovered so far links one of these cops to the local gangs."

"You're right." Reed abruptly shut the laptop and shot to his feet. "I guess this is why I'm not a detective."

"That's not what I meant," she protested. "If you were formally working this case as a detective, you'd have access to key information. We're limited as to what we can do via social media."

"Spinning our wheels with nothing to show for it." He sounded dejected. "Maybe we should take a walk."

"I wish we could." She'd have liked nothing more than to get out of their room.

Reed's phone rang, and he pounced on it as if it were a lifeline, putting it on speaker for her sake. "Carmichael."

"It's Brady Finnegan." Her brother's voice sounded low and tense, as if he were speaking quietly so no one else could overhear. "Doug was able to confirm that your Captain Jake Adams was the one who requested some of the officers from your district to participate on the task force."

"And he was also there the night of the shooting, which is unusual for him," Reed said, his gaze locked on hers. "Adams might be our guy."

"I don't know that you can go there yet," Brady cautioned. "Sounds like Adams deferred to Lieutenant Harvey as to which officers to use. Tate Brown was one of them, but there's another officer on the task force too. Guy by the name of Doyle Ford."

She sucked in a breath. "Doyle Ford was also there the night of the original shooting. He's one of the cops who transferred from the police department in Steven's Point."

"And why is that significant?" Brady asked.

"It probably isn't." Reed jumped into the three-way

conversation. "I was just making a note that two of the cops at the scene of the original shooting were transfers from other precincts."

"Not much gang activity in Steven's Point," Brady said. "Could be that since Doyle was new to the Milwaukee area, he was considered an asset to the task force."

"Really?" She frowned. "I would think that the opposite would be true. That a cop who knew the city inside and out would be better suited to be included."

Reed nodded slowly. "Alanna is right. I'm getting the impression the task force was set up to fail."

"I don't like it," Brady muttered. "We have experienced agents involved on our end. Why wouldn't MPD do the same?"

"Maybe because Adams didn't want it to succeed." Reed's voice was grim. "Can you get more information on Jake Adams for us?"

"Even a fed can't get police personnel files without a subpoena," Brady replied. "But I'll talk this through with Bridges in more detail, see what we can come up with."

"We need something to do," Alanna said, hoping she didn't sound as desperate as she felt. "Sitting around with nothing but possibilities swirling through our minds is driving us insane."

"What about the safe house you were working on?" Reed asked.

"I worked with Tarin to get access to the safe house he used a few months ago, when Faye and Colin were in danger," Brady said. "Grab a pen and paper, I'll give you the address and the code to get in."

Reed jotted the address on a piece of hotel stationery. Alanna swallowed a sigh, feeling as if they were giving up one set of prison walls for another.

"I'm serious, Brady. There must be something we can do to help." She met Reed's concerned gaze and shrugged. "Don't look at me like that. You're bored sitting around here too."

"True," Reed agreed. "Could we set up a meeting with Doyle Ford before heading to the safe house? I'd like to know what he remembers from the night of the shooting. Especially as it relates to Wesley Durango's murder."

"Maybe." Brady didn't sound enthusiastic. "The last time we set up a meeting, a cop got killed."

"I was hoping you or Doug Bridges would set up the meeting with Ford directly. Without going through the chain of command," Reed said. "I wouldn't want Lieutenant Harvey or Captain Adams knowing anything about it."

"Hang on a minute." There were muffled voices in the background before Brady returned. "Doug will set something up with Ford, making it clear this is not to go through official channels."

Alanna tried not to look too excited. "Great. When and where?"

"We're thinking of joining you at the City Center Hotel," Brady said. "Stay where you are, and we'll give you a time frame of our arrival when we know more."

"Thanks, Brady. I hope you can make the arrangements soon." Reed reached over to disconnect from the call.

"Do you really think your captain is involved?" Hard to imagine Rhy stooping so low.

"Maybe." Reed stared out the window for a long moment. "It seems almost too obvious. Anyone with an ounce of intelligence would put two and two together and come up with four."

"Rhy says criminals aren't always smart; otherwise, the

cops wouldn't catch so many of them," she pointed out. "They make mistakes, just like everyone else."

"Yeah, but a cop who has turned criminal has a lot to lose, so that individual would take extra precautions to hide the truth. Adding layers to protect them from being discovered and ratted out." Reed shook his head. "Then again, most cops don't go so far as to shoot their fellow officers either."

Alanna swallowed hard. She hoped and prayed they would find out more information from Doyle Ford.

She couldn't bear the thought of hitting yet another dead end. Literally or figuratively.

REED DUCKED out of the living area of the suite, desperate to go someplace where Alanna's enticing scent wouldn't wreak havoc with his concentration.

The way she talked about her family made him think of his older brother, Eric. He needed to reach out to his brother once this was over. Maybe they didn't have the same close-knit family ties of the Finnegans, but that didn't mean he couldn't try to change things. To stay connected.

Yet as much as he admired Alanna, becoming emotionally attached wasn't healthy. He couldn't take much more of this constant togetherness.

At least he had the upcoming meeting with Doyle Ford to help distract him.

After using the bathroom and splashing cold water on his face, he joined Alanna. He found her writing on a slip of paper. She glanced up as he approached. "Oh, there you are. I'm starting a list of questions for Doyle Ford."

"Let me see what you have so far." He tugged the paper

from beneath her fingers. She'd covered things like what did he know about Tate Brown's informant, Javier Patron. And about the task force in general. Since she'd covered what he would have, he slid it back to her. "I want to know where Ford was when Garcia was being tended to by the ambulance crew too. And roughly what time he last saw my partner alive."

She nodded, writing more notes. "What about learning more about why he transferred from Steven's Point?"

"Yeah, we can add that. Maybe get a feeling for how close he is to David Branch too. And whether or not he knows Olivia Baker."

"Okay." She wrote a few more notes, then handed the paper over. "I think those are a good place to start."

"If the meeting happens." The image of Tate Brown's dead body flashed in his mind.

"It will. Brady will follow through." Confidence in her brother shone in her warm brown eyes.

Surprisingly, he had as much faith in her family as she did. The only downside was that things weren't happening fast enough for him.

Remembering Nate's request to call him, he pulled out his disposable phone. He trusted Nate. Besides, using the disposable phone wouldn't lead anyone to the hotel. At least not easily.

To his surprise, Nate answered right away. "Hello?"

"Nate, it's Reed."

"Where are you?"

"Safe for now." He caught Alanna's concerned gaze and flashed a reassuring smile. "What have you heard? Are there rumblings of possible suspects we should be aware of?"

"Not that I know of, but I'm not in the Fifth Precinct

anymore." There was a pause, then Nate added, "I'm off today. Tell me where you are and I'll come pick you up. You need to keep your head down."

"Thanks for the offer, but I'm good. What I would like is for you to contact some of the guys from the fifth, see if you can learn anything. I need information more than anything else right now."

"Sure, I can do that. Are you sure you don't want me to pick you up?"

"I'm fine. But call me at this number if you get some intel, okay?"

"Okay," Nate agreed. "I'll be in touch."

"Thanks. Talk more later." He barely disconnected when Alanna pounced.

"Who was that? How do you know you can trust him?"

"He was my old partner and doesn't even work out of the fifth district anymore. Nate isn't involved in this. And he might learn something that can help."

Alanna didn't look convinced.

When his phone rang, he half expected the caller to be Nate, but it was Brady. "Hey, Doyle Ford returned our call. He's reluctantly agreed to meet us at City Central in thirty minutes. Wait for us in your suite. When Ford gets there, I'll escort him to your room, okay?"

"Fine. Just you, or Doug Bridges too?"

"Just me for now. Bridges is trying to find out the details of the conversation between our SAC and your chief of police. Sounds like everyone on the entire task force is being painted with the same guilty brush." There was a hint of disgust in Brady's tone. "Bridges is clean, but I can understand why everyone is on edge after the murder of Tate Brown."

"We'll see you soon, then." He put the phone in his

pocket and filled Alanna in. "The upper brass has their undies in a bundle over the murder outside the FBI offices. They're looking hard at the task force members."

"So they should. Two dead officers in less than twenty-four hours, plus another one with a price on his head, should light a fire under all of them." She waved a hand. "Those of us on the front lines have seen the increase in gunshot victims coming in each and every day. Maybe the reason the crime rate is so high is because there are bad cops on the force, working against those of you who are trying to keep people safe."

"It's always a few bad ones that taint the rest of us." He hated, absolutely hated when a cop turned bad. Every time there was an unjustified shooting or some other evidence of a dirty cop, every good cop on the street suffered.

And risked being killed because of someone's displaced anger.

Brady called from the lobby ten minutes earlier than their designated meeting time. "Everything okay?" Reed asked, feeling wary.

"Yep. I'm watching for Doyle Ford. Knowing him, he'll show up early too."

Reed couldn't help but smile. He knew full well the goal was always to arrive prior to the meeting time, hopefully catching the other party off guard.

"I think he's here," Brady said. "This guy matches the picture on my phone. Hang tight."

Reed ended the call and crossed over to stand beside the door. He fully expected both Brady and Ford to be armed. He gestured to Alanna. "Please stay back until we're clear."

"You make it sound like he'll come through the door guns blazing," she grumbled. But she did as he asked by ducking into her bedroom doorway.

Five minutes later, there was a sharp rap on the door. Reed peered through the peephole and confirmed that both Brady and Doyle were standing there.

He opened the door cautiously. "Brady. Ford. Come in."

"Carmichael?" Ford looked surprised to see him. His fellow cop darted an accusing glance at Brady. "You didn't tell me we were meeting him."

"I needed to keep Carmichael's location a secret." Brady didn't apologize for his deception. "There's a slew of gang members anxious to kill him to get their hands on the cash, remember?"

Doyle had the grace to flush. "Yeah, I remember." Doyle Ford was younger than Reed by a couple of years, but Reed felt at least a decade older. Ford nodded. "Carmichael."

"Ford. Thanks for coming." Reed closed the door and slid the dead bolt home. "Have a seat. Alanna Finnegan is here too."

At the sound of her name, Alanna emerged from the bedroom. "It's nice to meet you, Officer Ford."

"Call me Doyle." The younger cop sat and faced the three of them. "This is about the task force." It wasn't a question.

"Yes." Brady sat back, letting Reed start first. "Let's go back to the night of the multiple shooting between the Blood Kings and Latino Hombres. Was that meeting known by the task force?"

"Not at all." Doyle didn't hesitate. "To be honest, I was angry we didn't know about it. In my opinion, our snitch was useless."

"And who was that?" Reed asked as if he didn't already know. From what Doug said, the snitch's name was a secret.

"Javier Patron." Doyle sneered. "I didn't trust him one little bit, but Tate insisted he was helping."

"Interesting Tate trusted you with that information. Did you meet with Javier too?" Reed tried to understand the dynamics.

"No, Tate was the only one to meet with him. We tried to keep the meetings under wraps, and that was easier to do with only one cop involved."

"So only you and Tate knew the snitch's name?" Doyle nodded. Reed continued, "Do you remember seeing Wesley Durango the night of the gang shooting?"

Doyle took a moment to think back. "I remember him being there, but I lost track of him at some point. I remember somebody saying the rookie was sent to the hospital to guard Garcia."

"My partner didn't go in the ambulance, and he ended up dead. I'm trying to get a sense of when he disappeared," Reed said. "If you can remember."

Again, Doyle thought for a moment, then slowly nodded. "The scene was chaos, but I think I saw Wes standing near the ambulance while the crew was working on Garcia."

It wasn't much, but he'd take it. "Who nominated you to the task force?"

"Captain Adams. He called me into his office, told me that he thought some new blood would add a different perspective." Doyle looked between Reed and Brady. "I'll confess, I thought I was in over my head. I've been in Milwaukee for two years, but the level of violent crime I've been exposed to is very different from what I was used to back in Steven's Point."

"I can imagine." Reed thought it was crazy to put new officers on the task force. "Do you know Olivia Baker?"

"Yeah, I know her. She was the first to transfer. Told me how much action she was seeing on the streets. She recruited me and Tate. She was cute but dated a lot of guys, so I stayed clear."

No surprise there. "And how close are you and David Branch?"

Doyle looked surprised at the question. "We go way back. We were in the academy together and roomed together too. We decided to transfer to the big city where we'd see more action." Doyle's eyes abruptly widened. "You don't suspect Davy of being involved, do you?"

"No, I don't." But Captain Adams was beginning to ring several bells for him. "You know Wesley Durango was murdered. And so was Tate Brown."

"What?" Doyle paled. "I knew about Wes, but Tate? How? When? Who killed him?"

"That's why we're talking to you," Brady said, speaking for the first time. "Tate Brown was coming to the FBI for an interview about the task force and was shot in the parking lot of our building."

Doyle jumped to his feet. "You think I'm next? That everyone on the task force is a target to be murdered?"

"Hold on, I didn't say that." Brady lifted his hand in protest. "But that was the main reason I asked you to come here alone, without reporting in to your superior."

"I didn't tell him, but I don't like this." Doyle rose and paced the room, dragging his hand through his bright-red hair. "I should have stayed in Point," he muttered.

Reed understood how the guy felt. It was one thing to head into dangerous situations, but it was something very different to be targeted for execution.

"I have to go." Doyle abruptly turned and headed for the door. Reed jumped up to follow.

"Hang on, we have a few more questions."

Doyle ignored him. He wrenched the door open and swiftly headed for the side exit. The same one Reed and Alanna had used.

"Doyle, wait. You're safer with us," Reed said, running to catch up. But Doyle was running, too, and hit the door to bolt outside as if the devil himself was hot on his heels.

As Reed reached the door, the crack of gunfire echoed loudly, followed by the sound of glass shattering.

Reed instantly hit the ground, grimly realizing Ford must have been followed to City Central the same way a gunman had followed Tate Brown to the FBI building.

CHAPTER TWELVE

"Gunfire!" Brady leaped across the room and wrenched open the hotel room door, but then he glanced back at her. "Stay here."

She shook her head, quickly coming up behind him. "You might need me if someone is hurt."

Not Reed. Please, Lord, not Reed!

Brady didn't waste time arguing, no doubt fearing the worst. As she was.

Weapon in hand, Brady ran down the hall toward the open door. Peeking out from behind him, she raked her gaze over the area searching for Reed and Doyle.

But she didn't see anyone. Only shattered glass.

Wait, was that blood?

She sucked in a harsh breath but continued following Brady. Who was hit? Reed or Doyle?

Brady stopped when he reached the broken door. She lightly bumped into him from behind, grabbing her brother's arm to steady herself.

"Both men are down," Brady whispered.

No! Not Reed! She ruthlessly thrust her emotional response aside, focusing on what needed to be done.

"Cover me, Brady." She slipped around him. "I'll provide stabilizing medical care."

She could tell her brother didn't like it, but he gave a curt nod. "On three," he whispered.

While he counted down, she focused on the two men lying in the driveway along the side of the hotel. Reed was covering Doyle, which didn't surprise her. When Brady hit three, she burst out of the hotel as he fired into the air. The gunfire was incredibly loud, but her attention was focused on the two men on the asphalt.

Surrounded by blood.

"Get down," Reed said in a harsh whisper. "Call 911 to get an ambulance."

"Brady did. Are you hurt?"

"Doyle is worse." There was a hint of desperation in Reed's tone. "He took the brunt of the gunfire."

She nudged Reed aside. "Let me see his wound."

Reed reluctantly slid off his fellow officer. He didn't look at her but swept his gaze over the area where she assumed the gunfire had originated. "We can't stay long. I don't know if the shooter is still here."

Brady joined them, flanking her other side. "I'll run around to grab my SUV, okay? It will be safer to get you, Alanna, and Ford out of here."

"Hurry." Reed's voice held a note of desperation.

Alanna tried to tune them out as she palpated Doyle's entry wound. The front of his chest was awash in blood. The bullet had entered two inches to the left of Doyle's sternum. Close enough to have hit his heart.

The cop didn't appear to be breathing. She pressed her

fingers along his neck, searching for his carotid pulse, but felt nothing. His skin was already beginning to feel cool.

No pulse, no breathing. A gunshot wound to the chest. She could try CPR, but if the heart was damaged by a bullet, it would be impossible to keep blood circulating throughout his body. All efforts to revive him would be useless. She dropped her chin to her chest, hating the fact that there was nothing more she could do. Even surgery wouldn't help him now.

"He's gone," she whispered to Reed.

Reed's jaw tightened, but he didn't glance at her, never taking his eyes off the area surrounding them. "Stay down until Brady comes."

His flat, emotionless voice sent a warning chill down her spine. She was just as upset at knowing the body count of dead cops was up to three.

How many more until they figured out who was behind this?

She struggled to remain calm despite the tension radiating off Reed. A small pool of blood formed beneath his left arm. It took a second for her to realize his dark sleeve was soaked with blood.

Fresh blood, not from Doyle.

"You're hit!" Her voice came out louder than she intended. Reed still didn't turn to look at her.

"I'm fine, caught a bullet that ricocheted off the building." He tipped his head. "There's Brady. Get ready to jump inside."

"Not without you." Her gaze dropped to Doyle. "Are we leaving him here?"

"We have no choice. The cops who respond will arrange for him to be sent to the morgue." Reed clearly wasn't happy. Brady pulled up alongside them. "Go, Alanna."

"Get in the back with me so I can tend to your arm." Without waiting for his response, she wrenched open the back passenger door and crawled in.

Reed followed, slamming the door shut behind him. "Hit it, Brady."

In answer, her brother punched the gas, barreling down the side road past the shattered door until they were behind the building. Then Brady took the SUV up and over the curb, cutting in front of two other vehicles to reach the interstate.

"Brady, do you still have the first aid kit I made for you in here?" She palpated Reed's arm as best she could through the blood-soaked shirt sleeve.

"In the back." Brady met her gaze in the rearview mirror. "He's hit?"

"He can speak for himself," Reed said. "A minor wound on my upper arm."

"There's nothing minor about it." Alanna turned in her seat so she could reach into the back. When she found the large bin she'd put together years ago, she lifted it up and over to set it at her feet.

"That's a first aid kit?" Reed arched a brow. "Looks like a suitcase."

"You should be glad I made sure each of my siblings was prepared for an emergency like this." She opened the bin and rifled through to find what she needed. There were cleaning wipes, that she used on her hands. She then pulled out a bandage scissors along with several large pads. They were plastic on one side, while having an absorbent material on the other.

Placing one pad beneath his left arm, she used the scissors to cut away his sleeve. When Brady took a corner, causing her yank on the garment, a quick wince crossed Reed's features.

"Minor wound, huh?" She continued cutting the sleeve away until she could see the extent of his injury. When she noticed there was an entry wound but no exit wound, her gut tightened. "The bullet is still in your arm."

"Wrap it up, we can deal with it later."

"No, we can't. This will become infected. Brady, we need to get Reed to Trinity Medical Center."

"No." Reed's voice was harsh. "Gunshot wounds are an automatic report. I'm not putting the hospital staff in danger. I'm still a target, likely from someone inside the police department."

Brady sighed. "I tend to agree with Reed. Doyle was likely followed by the shooter."

She strove for patience. "I have a lot of supplies here, but no antibiotics. We need real medical care, not a slap and dash."

"Slap and dash will have to do for now." Reed's intense gaze held hers. "Do your best with what you have."

It wasn't nearly enough, but she did her best to attend to his wound. She opened a small bottle of sterile saline to clean the entry wound, then lightly packed it with gauze. "I can't remove the bullet while we're driving. If I'm jostled, I could push the bullet in farther or hit an artery or vein."

"That's fine." Reed didn't appear concerned. "Brady, are you heading for the safe house?"

"Yes, but only after I make sure we aren't being followed." Brady shook his head. "I can't believe Doyle is dead."

"Are we sure he didn't talk to his boss about meeting us?" Alanna finished wrapping Reed's arm, knowing this was a temporary fix. When they reached the safe house, she'd need to remove the bullet from his arm.

And figure out a way to get antibiotics for him. Without them, Reed would only have twenty-four to forty-eight hours before infection set it.

"I told him not to, and he claimed he didn't but who knows? Maybe he mentioned it to someone he shouldn't have." Brady sounded as tired as she felt.

"Either he talked to someone, or he was being watched," Reed said. "Based on his being involved in the task force, and the way he denied talking to anyone, it's likely the latter."

"He freaked out upon hearing of Tate Brown's death." She added an elastic wrap over the gauze dressing to add pressure. "Maybe he left because he knew he spoke to someone else within the task force."

"No way to know for sure until we get his phone records." Brady thumped his fist on the steering wheel. "This entire situation is unraveling at warp speed. And it still doesn't make any sense. Why risk killing so many cops?"

"Maybe the goal is to frame me," Reed said.

"No way," she protested, but Brady nodded slowly.

"Every time a cop was killed, you were nearby," Brady said. "Starting back when your rookie partner was murdered."

"Yeah. And for all we know, the target that's been put on my head didn't come from Garcia's gang members seeking revenge for his death," Reed continued. "The price could have come from the same dirty cop that set the task force up for failure."

"Dear Lord," she whispered, because now she could see the strong silky thread connecting each incident back to

Reed too. As if he were a fly captured in the middle of a spider's web.

And there didn't seem to be any way to escape.

THREE STRIKES *and you're out.*

From the beginning, Reed had wondered why the gunmen were hanging around outside his house. Even the price on his head had seemed an unusual undertaking for the Blood Kings.

But when Doyle Ford had been shot right in front of him, there had been no denying he alone was the common denominator. That once Reed had been shot and killed, evidence would be planted somewhere that would point to him as the bad cop. And after he was dead, there wouldn't be a way to clear his name.

When Ford had gone down, Reed had hit the ground too, then crawled on his belly to reach his fellow officer. He'd suspected the cop was dead but had protected him the best he could.

So much death and destruction. And for what? Money?

His left arm throbbed painfully. Maybe he should just put himself out there, sacrificing his life to prevent other innocent lives from being taken.

"I've made several turns." Brady's voice roused him from his dark thoughts. "I think we're in the clear to head to the safe house."

"Good. I need to get a better look at Reed's injury." Alanna tapped her giant first aid kit. "And a way to get antibiotics ASAP."

"I'll be fine." He understood her concern, but the way things were happening at the speed of light, this would be over long before infection had the chance to settle in. "We need to call Bridges. Two members of the task force are dead, and the rest of the team needs to be put on notice and stashed in safe houses too. Just because Doug is a fed doesn't mean he won't be targeted for elimination."

Brady touched the communication system. "Call Doug Bridges."

There was a ringing sound, then Doug's voice came through the speaker. "Brady? What's going on?"

"Doyle Ford was shot outside the side entrance of the City Central Hotel." Brady cut right to the chase. "Every member of the task force needs to go off-grid. Including you."

"How in the world did that happen?" Doug's tone was incredulous.

"We don't know if Doyle talked to someone despite your directive not to or if he was followed. What did you find out from the SAC?"

"Donovan told me he felt like he was getting the runaround from the chief. No straight answers but a lot of innuendo, especially related to Reed Carmichael."

"Shocking," Reed muttered.

"We think Reed is being set up to take the fall on these murders," Brady explained. "They all happened when he was nearby."

"Based on how fast we lost Doyle Ford, I can't argue." Doug paused, then added, "And maybe the price on your head didn't originate with the Blood Kings at all."

"Exactly," Brady agreed. "We've already figured out that the dirty cop managed to get the word out on the street about that."

"Regardless, we need a game plan," Alanna interjected.

"And fast. Having three dead cops is unacceptable. There must be a way for the FBI to pull rank on this."

"I'll see what I can do," Doug said. "We should be able to convince Donovan to put more FBI resources on this."

"Let's get Marc Callahan involved," Brady suggested. "We know we can trust him."

"He was asked to help dig through intel, but we need him now more than ever. Hang tight, I'll be in touch." Doug ended the call.

"I'm not sure adding another fed is a good idea," Reed said. "Bad enough you and Doug are in danger because of me."

"We're all invested in this, Carmichael, so get over it." Brady's voice was curt. "Marc Callahan will be a good asset for us."

Reed didn't doubt the guy's skill, but adding more innocent people to the mix didn't sit well with him.

"I agree, the more cops working on this, the better." Alanna turned in her seat to face him. "You're not alone. We're going to dig until we uncover who is behind this."

He grimaced, wishing he felt as positive about the inevitable outcome as she did.

"The safe house is up ahead," Brady said. "I'm going to drive past and circle around the block before pulling in."

"Great." Alanna looked relieved to have reached their destination. "I have an idea about how we can get the antibiotics. I'll contact our new sister-in-law."

Brady nodded. "Faye will help out without a problem."

"Who is Faye?" Reed tried to place the name.

"Faye Finnegan, Colin's wife. She's an emergency department physician. I should have thought of using her expertise earlier." Alanna sighed. "Blame it on the nonstop adrenaline rush."

"Will she get in trouble for helping me?" Reed met Brady's gaze in the rearview mirror. "I feel like I've caused enough trouble for the Finnegan family."

"I'm sure it will be fine," Alanna said, although the way she looked away was not convincing. "Once the danger is over, she can report the gunshot wound the way she's required to do by state law."

Reed knew full well Faye Finnegan was required to report gunshot wounds, and since the bullet was still lodged in his arm, he didn't see a way around it. "I'd rather you just take care of the wound, Alanna."

"You need antibiotics or risk losing your arm, maybe even your life." She had that stubborn Finnegan glint in her eye.

"Faye might be working today anyway," Brady said. "If so, she can't leave in the middle of her shift."

"I know." Alanna frowned. "Didn't she say something about working night shift this week?"

Brady shrugged. "I can barely keep our siblings' schedules straight, much less their spouses'."

"If she's on nights, she's probably sleeping, but I'll touch base with Colin. Maybe she can at least call in a prescription for Reed."

"I'm fine, let's just get to the safe house." He tried not to sound as cranky as he felt. His arm hurt like crazy, and he struggled with knowing yet another cop was brutally murdered.

His situation was getting worse, not better.

And there was no end in sight.

"Okay, here's the safe house." Brady pulled up to a nondescript brick building. He threw the gearshift into park, then turned in his seat to face them. "It doesn't look like much, but the glass is bullet resistant, and there are security cameras outside that will alert you to anyone getting close."

"That sounds promising." After the multiple shooters targeting him, he appreciated the bullet-proof glass. "Is the house stocked with any food?"

"Some canned goods," Brady said. "But I'll gladly pick up some groceries."

Reed wasn't the least bit hungry, but Alanna needed to eat. He pushed his door open and slid out, swallowing hard at the shaft of pain. "Get whatever Alanna wants."

Brady gave Alanna the code to the door, then covered them from behind as they made their way inside. The interior was plain and serviceable with none of the useless decorations that adorned most hotel rooms.

"I want you to stretch out on the bed in the closest bedroom," she directed. "Brady, bring in the first aid kit. No need to worry about groceries until we know if Faye will order antibiotics, as those will need to be picked up at the closest pharmacy as well."

"You need to eat." Reed hated feeling helpless, but he entered the first bedroom on the right-hand side of the hallway. He did as Alanna asked, stretching out so that she could access his injured left arm.

At least it wasn't his dominant hand. The situation would be worse if he couldn't shoot his weapon with any sort of accuracy.

Alanna went to work, lifting his arm to place several pads beneath it. Then she fetched towels and a washcloth from the bathroom. When she began rummaging in the large first aid kit, he tried to peer over the edge. "What are you looking for?"

"Sterile forceps and a penlight." She set them aside. "I'll

need to wash the wound with hydrogen peroxide, which is going to hurt." She met his gaze. "Very badly."

He tried to smile. "Can't be worse than getting shot."

"The surge of adrenaline that you experienced in the middle of the shooting would have dulled the pain." She captured her lower lip between her teeth. "I hate knowing I'll hurt you, but I need to get that bullet out right away."

"I'll manage. Go ahead and do your thing."

"In a minute." She glanced over her shoulder. "Brady? Did you get in touch with Colin?"

"He didn't answer, but I left a message, specifically asking for antibiotics from Faye. Hopefully, he'll call back soon." Brady entered the room, his gaze assessing the scene. "Do you need my help?"

"Yes, hold the penlight." She opened many packets of gauze, setting them nearby. Then she took a moment to remove the dressing she applied in the car. Her gaze finally met his. "Are you ready?"

He nodded, curling his right hand into a fist to brace himself. "Go for it."

Her brow furrowed as she donned a pair of gloves and dipped the washcloth into the warm solution of hydrogen peroxide and water. The pain was worse than he'd anticipated. He squeezed his eyes shut and took several deep breaths as she thoroughly cleaned the wound.

His stomach clenched with nausea, and he could feel sweat popping out on his forehead. He didn't complain and oddly found himself reciting the only prayer he remembered from his childhood days of attending church as a distraction.

"I'm sorry," Alanna whispered, obviously seeing his discomfort. "Brady, hold the penlight up a little higher. Reed, I need to extract bullet."

If he'd thought the pain he'd endured earlier was bad, this was far worse.

Instead of saying the Lord's Prayer, he silently screamed in his mind. He must have blacked out because the next thing he knew, Alanna was hovering over him.

"Reed? Can you hear me?"

"Yes." His voice was barely a whisper through his tight throat. "Go ahead, I'm okay. Finish up."

The furrow between her brows deepened. "I already took the bullet out and dressed the wound." She rested her hand on his forearm. "You had me worried when you didn't respond to my voice."

Turning his head, he looked at the clean, fresh gauze that she'd wrapped around his arm. "Where's the slug?"

"Brady took it for evidence." She still seemed concerned. "I found a bottle of ibuprofen, but I'd rather not give it to you on an empty stomach."

His stomach still churned, so he didn't argue. "How long?" He cleared his throat. "How long have I been out?"

"Twenty minutes." She sank into a chair she'd placed near his bed. "Faye is heading into work tonight, but she called in a prescription for antibiotics. Brady went to pick it up along with some groceries."

"Good." He shifted on the bed, sending another wave of pain radiating down his left arm. It wasn't so bad if he didn't move, but lying here doing nothing wasn't an option. "Help me up."

"What? No way." She pressed down on his forearm. "You need to recover. Most people are well medicated with narcotics when they have a foreign object removed."

"We need a plan. To find the dirty cop responsible for this mess." Despite his determination to get up, he couldn't seem to force his body to do his bidding.

"Please, Reed." Her brown gaze held a mix of pleading and compassion. "I'm going to heat a bowl of canned soup I found in the cupboard. Once Brady returns with groceries and the antibiotics, you'll need to take a dose along with some ibuprofen. Both need to be taken on a full stomach."

"Okay." He tried to relax. Brady would make sure he wasn't followed. The three of them were the only ones who knew the address of the safe house.

Unless Brady had shared the information with Doug Bridges.

"I'll be back." She surprised him by leaning over to lightly brush her lips against his. The kiss was so brief he thought he might have imagined it, especially since she quickly left the room.

Reed stared up at the ceiling, wishing for the chance to kiss Alanna again. A proper kiss this time. But even as the thought of seeing more of her at some point entered his mind, he knew it was a bad idea.

For the first time since killing Ivan Garcia, Reed understood his chances of getting out of this alive were slim to none.

The dirty cop would either kill him or plant enough evidence that he'd end up going to prison. And since cops didn't do well in prison, he didn't harbor any illusions about his chances of making it through any sort of confinement unscathed.

From what he could tell? Either way, he was a dead man.

CHAPTER THIRTEEN

Despite the chill in the house, she was sweating as she opened several cans of chicken noodle soup, a Finnegan go-to when sick. As she put the bowl in the microwave, she realized her fingers were trembling. She closed the door and set the timer for two and a half minutes, then braced herself on the counter, praying she wouldn't fall.

Digging the bullet from Reed's arm had been more difficult than she'd imagined. Even after he'd passed out, she couldn't relax. The pathetic beam of the penlight hadn't been nearly good enough to see. She'd had to poke around to find and remove the slug, battling nausea every step of the way.

And this was why she wasn't a surgeon.

Pushing away from the counter, she walked from window to window, fighting for control. She'd done it. If she were honest, she'd admit that without Brady's calm, confident voice urging her on, she may not have been able to continue removing the bullet. Her brother was a rock, and she owed him big-time for his help.

She wanted to believe the worst was over, but it wasn't. Working in the ED had shown her how fast an infection could turn to septic shock.

And how deadly it could be.

The loud ding of the microwave startled her so badly she spun around, whacking her hip sharply against the counter.

She managed to remove the bowl of soup without spilling any. Then she looked for a tray, forced to settle for using a cutting board.

Feeling stronger, she carried the makeshift tray to Reed's bed. When she noticed the bed was empty, she frowned.

"Reed?" She hastily set the tray on the end table, then made her way around the bed, fearing he'd rolled onto the floor. Thankfully, he wasn't lying there in a crumpled heap. Hearing the toilet flush brought an inordinate sense of relief.

Of course, he was in the bathroom.

She needed to get a grip. What happened to being cool under pressure?

Reed emerged, looking pale with pain bracketing his mouth but strong enough that he wasn't hanging on to the wall for support. "Hey. Thought I heard the microwave."

"Do you need help?" She automatically went into nurse mode, crossing over to put her arm around his waist to guide him across the room. "Can you sit up in the bed?"

"I'm not eating soup in bed." He stopped, eyeing her with the obstinate look she'd come to recognize. "I'll eat in the kitchen so I don't make a mess."

Biting back a protest, she threw her hands up. "Fine. I'll carry the tray back."

At least he didn't try to take it from her. She could tell he was in pain, but he hid it well, moving slowly but surely down the hallway to the kitchen. He sank into the closest chair as if he couldn't put up the pretense for much longer.

"Start with the soup. Brady will be here soon with the groceries." She set the bowl of soup in front of him and returned the cutting board to the counter. "Let's say grace, if you don't mind. Despite losing Doyle Ford, we have a lot to be thankful for."

"I'd like that," Reed murmured.

She nodded and sat beside him. "Dear Lord, we thank You for this food we are about to eat. Please heal Reed's wound. We also ask that You continue to keep us all safe from harm, while granting us the strength and wisdom we need to seek justice."

"Amen," Reed said.

"Amen." She sat for a moment, truly grateful they were still alive, even though she mourned the loss of another cop's life.

Then she jumped up. "Oh, I have some ibuprofen for you too." She opened the bottle she'd left on the counter and removed four tablets.

"Four?" He frowned. "That's too much."

"Trust me, we often give patients eight hundred milligrams for severe pain." She wished she had something stronger to offer. "And I doubt this amount will come close to making you feel better."

Reed grunted and took a few sips of the soup. She watched him closely but didn't get the sense he was about to throw up.

By the time he finished the soup, Brady returned with groceries and, more importantly, the antibiotics. "Thanks,

Brady. You, stay there." She pointed a finger at Reed when it looked like he was about to stand. "Toast is coming up."

"I ate the soup." He scowled, looking like a kid who didn't want to finish his vegetables.

"And you'll eat the toast too. Then we'll get the first dose of antibiotics in your system." Oddly, she felt better having him sitting at the table and arguing with her. That moment he'd lost consciousness from the pain she'd inflicted upon him still haunted her.

"Is she always this bossy?" Reed asked.

"Not as bad as Rhy." Brady shrugged as he put the food away. "She gets like this when we're hurt or sick." Her brother grinned. "Don't you feel sorry for her patients?"

"What are you talking about? My patients love me." She paused, then added, "Well, most of them." Garcia was clearly an exception.

While Reed ate toast, she reviewed the information sheet that accompanied the antibiotics. Then she opened the bottle and dropped a large horse pill into her hand. Refilling the cup of water, she gave them to Reed. "One pill three times a day. We'll sneak in a second dose before bed."

"What are the side effects?" Reed tossed the pill back and gulped water.

"Most commonly an upset stomach. Which is why I forced you to eat toast and soup." She eyed him warily. "Ready to head back to your room?"

"No, I need to talk to Brady about a game plan. We can't sit around here forever." Reed frowned as her brother pulled out a frozen pizza and preheated the oven. "How come I get toast and soup while you guys get pizza?"

"Because you're an invalid," Brady said with mock seriousness.

"You can have some. Just don't puke up those antibiotics or you'll be taking a one-way trip to the hospital."

"Bossy," Reed muttered.

Once the pizza was in the oven, Brady took a seat across from Reed. She sat between them, determined to be a part of whatever cockamamy plan they came up with.

"First I'd like to know if Doug Bridges has given you any more information." Reed leaned forward, resting his injured arm on the table. "Not just on the recent shooting, but anything since this nightmare started."

"I think I told you about the meeting between the chief and our SAC," Brady said. "Doug and Marc Callahan were able to convince our boss that there is definitely a dirty cop pulling the strings. Likely someone on or involved with setting up the task force."

She fought a wave of frustration. "We already know that."

"Us knowing it and the special agent in charge believing it are two different things," Brady pointed out. "And we still don't have proof to back up our suspicions."

"I'm glad your boss is on board, but we need to figure out who this guy is before he kills another cop." Reed's voice was strong, but she noticed his energy was flagging. Considering he basically went through a minor surgical procedure without the benefit of sedation, she was surprised he was still upright.

"Donovan is calling his boss for more resources." Brady lifted a hand when Reed rolled his eyes. "Look, I know you're sick of talking and want action, but we can't take down a dirty cop without help. And frankly, you need rest. You look as if you're about to fall off that chair."

"I'm fine." Reed grimaced. "Or I will be once the ibuprofen kicks in. Let's review what we've learned so far."

Alanna nodded, glancing at her brother. "We found a few connections that you should know about. First Doyle Ford, David Branch, and Olivia Baker are all MPD officers who transferred in from Steven's Point."

Brady frowned. "You think that's significant?"

"We don't know. But Wesley has a picture of himself standing with Olivia Baker on his social media page." Reed hesitated, then added, "I dated Olivia for several months."

"Did you part on bad terms?" Brady asked.

"No, we agreed we wanted different things out of our lives. Doyle mentioned she gets around, and I'm not surprised by that. There're too many connections to be a coincidence."

"True." Brady sighed. "What else?"

"I spoke briefly to my former partner, Nate Jackson. He doesn't work out of my precinct anymore, but he offered to help dig up information." Reed grimaced. "He's off today, so we should keep that in mind if we need additional assistance."

"I'm still trying to understand the connection between three cops who once worked out of Steven's Point." Brady scowled, then rose and checked the pizza. "It's not like Point is a hotbed of crime."

"Yes, but then why put Tate Brown and Doyle Ford on the task force?" Reed asked. "Two guys that are new to the area? That's really bugging me."

"I understand and share your concern," Brady said. "By the way, I let Rhy know we're safe. He's staying with Devon at the hospital overnight. Elly will be at the homestead with Colin since Faye is working night shift."

"Good." She swept a critical eye over Reed. "I'll let you have one slice of pizza as long as you promise not to puke and that you'll go back to bed."

"Okay." The fact that Reed didn't argue was a bit concerning. Yet she also knew he was the type to test his limits.

When the pizza was ready, Brady pulled the pie from the oven, sliced it, and set it on the center of the table. He said grace since he hadn't been there earlier. To her surprise, Reed didn't seem to mind.

She placed the smallest slice on a plate for Reed, then helped herself.

They ate in silence. She had to admit, Reed seemed to tolerate the pizza pretty well. But he didn't ask for another slice, pushing his plate away when he was finished.

"I think someone should go to my house, as I'm fairly certain incriminating evidence will end up there." Reed sighed and rubbed the back of his neck with his uninjured arm. "If it hasn't been planted already."

Her stomach clenched. It was difficult to fathom that evidence pointing to Reed would be planted in his home, but three cops were dead.

There was no limit to what this guy would do.

"I've considered heading over," Brady said slowly. "But I don't want to leave you here when you're wounded. And honestly, it doesn't matter if they planted evidence. Not now that the feds are involved."

"I can ask Nate to do that for me since he offered to help." Reed grimaced as he stood. "I'll call him."

"Good idea," Brady said.

She jumped up and slipped her arm around his waist. "Lean on me."

"I'm fine." But he moved slowly as if needing all his concentration to stay upright, putting one foot in front of the other.

When they reached the bedroom, she stayed close by as

he carefully sat on the edge of the bed. "Make your call, then get some rest. I'll wake you at midnight with more toast and your second dose of antibiotic."

"If you insist." He offered a small smile. "Seriously, Alanna, thanks. I appreciate what you did for me."

"You saved my life." She watched as he winced while stretching out on the bed. "The least I can do is to try to save yours."

"Angel of mercy," he whispered as he closed his eyes. She instinctively pulled the covers over him and had to resist the urge to kiss him again.

He was her patient, nothing more. And she was worried she'd already done enough damage by not insisting he go to the hospital for proper treatment.

She prayed he wouldn't suffer permanent damage because of her decision.

REED BARELY REMEMBERED when Alanna woke him at midnight to feed him toast, more ibuprofen, and the awful horse pill.

But by morning, he felt better. Not great, but good enough to get down to the business of figuring out who was responsible for killing three good cops.

How? That was the kicker. He had no idea.

Since he couldn't shower, he made do with sticking his head under the sink to wash his hair one-handed. He was forced to do everything one-handed, and that wasn't good. It worried him that he didn't have the range of motion he needed in his injured arm. There was little he could do but continue to pray God would give him strength when he needed it.

Moving silently, he made his way to the kitchen. His stomach didn't feel great, but he figured that was from the antibiotic. He shouldn't have given Alanna grief about forcing him to eat toast. She obviously knew what she was doing.

He was glad to see one of the Finnegans, probably Alanna, had set up the coffeemaker last night. All he had to do was push the button. As he watched the machine begin to brew, he thought about the message he'd left his former partner last night. Nate hadn't answered his call, so he'd left a message about heading to his place to see if there was evidence planted there that would be used against him.

"Good morning."

He spun at the sound of Alanna's husky voice, his hand going to his gun. Then he relaxed. "I didn't hear you come in."

Her smile widened. "I heard you bumping around in the bathroom. I'm glad you're up, though. I need to take another look at your arm."

"Not until I have coffee." He didn't relish the thought of a dressing change. "Thanks for setting it up ahead of time."

"You're welcome." She opened the fridge. "How about eggs and toast for breakfast?"

"That would be great." He'd thought sharing a house would feel less intimate than being in the hotel suite. But it wasn't.

Not by a long shot.

He poured coffee for them, pushing the cream and sugar toward her. He tried to stay out of her way as she prepared breakfast.

Hearing someone coming down the hall made him sigh in relief. Thank goodness for Brady.

"Yeah, I'm up. Hang on, I want to put you on speaker so

Reed can hear this too." Brady entered the kitchen and placed his phone on the table. Alanna turned away from the stove to come join them, bringing a cup of coffee for her brother who took it gratefully. "Okay, Marc. We're all here. Tell us what you know."

"Donovan talked to his boss, and they're opening a formal investigation into the joint task force we have with the MPD and the key people within the police department that may be involved."

He tried not to show his annoyance with the feds doublespeak. "Tell us who exactly you guys are looking at."

There was a pause, then Marc said, "The chief himself, all the way down to your boss, Lieutenant Harvey."

"That's way too many layers," Reed protested. "You need to narrow it down. Why not start with Lieutenant Harvey and Captain Adams?"

"The only leadership level they've completely cleared is your sergeant, Noah Sinclair. Not just because he's my brother-in-law, but when Doug interviewed him, he was completely shocked to hear about the task force. And that two of his officers were involved."

Brady shook his head. "I'm sure Noah was not happy to be kept in the dark."

"He wasn't," Marc agreed.

Reed could understand why. "I still think Captain Adams should be our top suspect. He never goes to crime scenes, preferring to sit in his office, but he was there the night of the shooting and of course came to the hospital." The more Reed thought about it, the more convinced he was that Adams could have taken Wesley aside and had him killed without any of the other cops noticing. "He must have thought it was important to be there. Not to support his officers, but for some other reason."

"Like what?" Brady asked.

He raked his hand through his hair. "I don't know. Maybe he knew there was some big deal going down that night. And somehow the Latino Hombres found out about the deal, too, so they showed up. There were so many people, cops and gang members, it was difficult to keep track of what was happening."

"Okay, I'll send that information up to our SAC," Marc said. "The only concern I have about Adams as a suspect is how he connected with the gangs in the first place, considering he does sit in his office."

"I know, but that brings up Lieutenant Harvey. He transferred from Chicago a few years ago. We all know the Milwaukee gang activity started with several gang members from Chicago escaping to start over here."

"Another good point," Marc agreed. "I'll pass that tidbit along too."

"Is there anything else we can do to help?" Brady asked. "We have a computer, and we'd like to put it to good use."

"I'll get back to you on that. For now, keep your head down. I'll let you know if anything else comes up."

Reed caught Brady's gaze. "Okay, thanks, Marc."

"That was disappointing," Alanna said. She rose and crossed to the fridge. The scent of bacon already wafted toward them. "Brady, I'm making eggs over easy, toast, and bacon. Afterward, I'll need to change Reed's dressing."

"Sounds good." Brady turned back to him. "Think back to the past few weeks. Has your captain acted out of the ordinary in other ways?"

It was a good question. Reed ignored the throbbing in his arm and tried to go back over the past few weeks. He didn't interact with the captain on a daily basis, but he vaguely remembered his partner mentioning a strange inter-action with the captain.

What had Wesley said?

"Wes told me he was walking past Adam's office when he saw two officers step out. Both guys looked as if they'd gotten their butts chewed out over something they'd done. And Wes wondered why the two cops were in the office together since they weren't partners on the job." He shook his head ruefully. "I wish I'd asked more questions, but I didn't. I can't help wondering if the captain had spoken to the two guys on the task force."

"You mean the two officers who are now dead," Brady clarified. "Doyle Ford and Tate Brown."

He frowned. "Yeah, I wish I could say that those two were the cops Wesley saw with certainty, but I can't. You asked about unusual activity with Adams, and Wes thought the meeting was strange." He couldn't help wondering if Wesley had seen something that fateful night. During the chaos that ensued after the shooting, had his partner witnessed something going down between Adams and a member of the Blood Kings gang?

Was that the reason he'd been killed and stuffed in their squad?

"What?" Brady asked. "I can see the wheels in your mind spinning."

"Just wondering if Wesley saw Adams with a gang member the night of the shooting. It would explain why he was murdered." He met Brady's gaze. "It never occurred to me before now, but maybe I was being set up to take the fall long before I shot Garcia."

"This case makes my head hurt," Brady muttered.

"Breakfast will be ready in a few minutes." Alanna brought the pot over to refill their mugs.

"Thanks." Reed gave her a small smile. "I'm sure it's time for another horse pill."

"It is." She replaced the coffeepot, then brought the antibiotic and ibuprofen bottles over.

Five minutes later, three plates full of food were set on the table. Alanna dropped into the chair beside him.

"I'll say grace," Brady offered. He bowed his head. "Dear Lord, we thank You for this food and for the protection offered by this safe house. We ask that You continue to guide us on the path to truth and justice. Amen."

"Amen," Reed echoed.

"Amen," Alanna added. Then she grinned. "Dig in."

The food tasted wonderful and settled his stomach. A situation he was sure would change once he'd downed the antibiotic. They were quiet as they ate, digesting the recent conversation with Marc Callahan. Once he'd finished his meal, he swallowed the horse pill and ibuprofen.

When his disposable phone rang, two pairs of brown eyes bored into him. He glanced at the screen, recognizing Nate's number. "My former partner," he explained, before taking the call. "Nate? What's going on?"

"I found a wad of cash and drugs inside your house," Nate whispered. "I barely got out of there before several squads pulled in."

His gut clenched. "Did you take the evidence with you?"

"Yeah, that's why you asked me to go over, isn't it? Can we meet so I can hand it over?" Nate sounded as if he were on edge. "I don't want to be caught with this stuff."

"Yes, we'll meet. Get out of there for now. I'll call you back in a few minutes."

"Okay, thanks." His former partner disconnected from the call.

"What evidence?" Brady asked.

"Money and drugs." Even as he said the words and had expected something like this, Nate's blunt statement was a shock.

He was being set up as the dirty cop to protect the real bad guy.

CHAPTER FOURTEEN

"Why did you agree to meet with him?" Alanna stared at Reed. "We can't bring him here to the safe house."

Reed frowned. "Didn't you hear what he said? Money and drugs were planted at my house! Nate was kind enough to take it out of there. He can't keep it." He turned to Brady. "The feds need to log the evidence and hang on to it."

"Hold on, Reed." Brady lifted a hand. "I get you want that stuff out of your house, but you must realize there's no chain of custody here. Only your buddy's word that he took it from your home."

Alanna shot her brother a grateful look. "I agree, we shouldn't rush to trust this guy."

Reed narrowed his gaze. "Nate is my former partner, not some random guy. He doesn't work out of my precinct any longer, which is how I got paired up with the rookie."

"I don't know." She gnawed on her lower lip. "What do you think, Brady? I mean, this guy is a cop. He can document chain of custody, can't he?"

Her brother wasn't convinced. "He can, but there

wasn't anyone with him to corroborate where the drugs and money were found, right?"

Reed hesitated, glancing at his phone. "Not that he mentioned, although I'm sure he took pictures. But you need to understand, I'm the one who asked him to go to my place to check. Nate did that as a favor to me. It's not fair to keep him hanging in the wind. He's married. There's no way he wants to take drugs and dirty cash home."

Alanna didn't like where this was headed. Especially when Brady nodded.

"Yeah, I can see how that's a problem." He sighed. "Fine, we'll arrange a meeting, but not here. We need to keep the location of this place a secret."

"I agree, and thanks, Brady." Reed's expression was grim. "I know this may not help much in the long run, especially if there's other stuff planted there that Nate wasn't able to find, but it's a step forward in thwarting the bad guy's plan to hang me out to dry."

"That only works if there wasn't evidence left behind that Nate missed. Even a small amount of evidence could be detrimental. Why risk leaving the safe house to take it from Nate's hands?" Alanna asked.

"Because Nate did me a favor, that's why." A muscle at the corner of his mouth ticked. "There's no reason to make him suffer because some dirty cop is determined to frame me for his misdeeds."

"Can't Nate drop the drugs and money off somewhere? We can pick it up later, then, right?" Alanna pressed.

"That would negate any attempt at keeping a semblance of chain of custody," Brady said.

She didn't care, but as she glanced between Reed and Brady, their determined expressions confirmed they'd already decided to move forward with meeting Reed's former partner. "I'm going on record that I think this is a bad idea."

"Noted," Reed spoke in a curt tone. The hardness in his blue eyes made her realize he thought she wasn't being supportive.

She leaned forward to capture his hand. "Reed, I don't like it that evidence was found at your house, and I understand you want to clear your name. But don't you see? None of that will matter if you're dead."

"We'll take precautions." Brady's tone was reassuring. "No one is going to die today."

"Famous last words," she grumbled. When Reed didn't say anything more, she sighed and stood, releasing him. Two seasoned cops against one nurse meant her opinion was overruled. "I'll clean up the kitchen."

"I need to call Nate back. How much time do we need to set up a meeting?" Reed asked.

"I'd like a solid two hours." Brady scratched his chin. "Let Nate know we'll call him back with a time and place, but be vague. I'm sure he won't be happy to know this won't be happening soon."

"I will," Reed agreed. As he reached for his phone, Brady left the room, presumably to make backup arrangements with Marc and Doug.

Alanna listened to Reed's side of the brief conversation. "Nate? I need a little time before we can meet." There was a pause before Reed continued. "I know this is important. And I owe you for this. But with the price on my head, I've been flying under the radar. I don't have ready access to a vehicle. I need to get my hands on a car."

Reed listened for several seconds before thanking Nate for his patience and ending the call. She glanced over her shoulder to find Reed staring pensively at the phone.

"What's wrong?"

He lifted his head. "Nothing. Nate is really anxious to meet with me. Says having the evidence in his possession makes him feel like a criminal."

The tingle of unease wouldn't leave her alone. "Please don't do this."

"I have to." Reed grimaced as he rose to his feet. "I'm sure your brother will have the area well covered with feds."

She trusted Brady, Marc, and Doug too. Doing her best to shake off the feeling of impending doom, she quickly washed their breakfast dishes. When Reed came over and picked up a towel, she shook her head. "No point in trying to dry dishes with one hand. We'll let them air dry."

"I'm not an invalid."

"Maybe not, but you're being ridiculous to push the issue." She snatched the towel from his hand. "If you're so determined to have this meeting, it would be smart to get some rest."

He shot her an annoyed look but turned and headed toward the hallway leading to the bedrooms. She dropped her chin to her chest for a moment, then lifted her eyes to the sky outside the window.

Please, Lord Jesus, keep us all safe in Your care.

The prayer helped calm her nerves. Maybe she was making a mountain out of an ant hill. She filled her coffee mug, then crossed into the living room where Brady was seated on the sofa, his phone next to him. She set her coffee down, then dropped beside him.

"Hey, don't look so worried." Her brother lightly punched her shoulder. "We've got this. Marc and Doug are going to get to the meeting site early. Reed will have plenty of backup."

"I know." She forced a smile. "It just seems like an unnecessary risk."

Her brother shrugged. "If one of our family members had done a favor and needed to get rid of evidence to protect themselves, we wouldn't let anything, or anyone, hold us back."

She hated to admit he was right. "This guy isn't Reed's family."

"A cop's partner is family, sis," Brady said gently. "No question about that."

"Funny, but I get the sense that Rhy, Tarin, Kyleigh, and you all place our blood ties well above your cop family."

Brady smiled. "True. But Reed doesn't have eight Finnegan siblings. Cops trust their partners to have their backs. Don't give Reed a hard time about this."

Too late, she thought sadly. She already had.

Brady's phone rang. He picked it up and answered, "Hi, Marc. Did you and Doug decide on a place for the meeting?"

Alanna leaned forward trying to hear the other side of the conversation.

"Okay, I like that idea. Especially if there's plenty of trees around to keep you both covered. I'll get Reed to set up the meeting with his partner at ten-thirty, sixty minutes from now. I'll let you know how it goes. Later." He lowered the phone.

"Where are you meeting?" Alanna asked.

"Greenland Park, not far from the swing sets." Brady grinned. "I'm very familiar with the area since it's Caleb's favorite place to go."

"I thought that's the park where Caleb escaped his kidnapper? Why on earth would you take him back there?"

"The counselor suggested it as a way to replace the bad

memories with good ones, since he was rescued from there too." Brady shrugged. "It's working. Caleb hasn't had a nightmare about the kidnapping in the past three months."

"Okay, Greenland Park." She wished she was as familiar with the area. "Will Reed's partner view the location as a setup?"

"It's not a setup," Brady argued. "It's a way to provide cover should Reed need it. If Nate simply hands over the evidence and leaves, he'll never know Marc and Doug were there. If he doesn't . . ." He shrugged. "Then he'll get the full wrath of the bureau."

"Okay." She threw up her hands. "But I'm going too."

He frowned. "Not a good idea."

"Too bad. Reed isn't at one hundred percent with his injury. If something happens, and this meeting goes south, I want to be nearby to render aid. We'll bring the first aid kit too."

"Fine, but you'll need to stay in the car." Brady lifted a hand when she was about to argue. "Don't push me on this or I'll drop you off by Rhy."

"He's at the hospital with Devon." She winced. "Which reminds me, I better call to see how she's doing."

"You do that. I'm going to talk to Reed. We'll leave here in fifteen to twenty so we're there ahead of his partner."

She nodded, understanding the logic. She quickly called Rhy, thankful he answered. "How is she?"

"Good, but the contractions started up again last night." Rhy sounded exhausted and concerned. "The doc wants to watch her one more day."

"I'm sorry, but it's for the best. She's in good hands."

"I know." Hearing the strain in his tone, she wished she could give him a hug. "Thanks for checking in. I'll let you know if we're able to head home."

"You do that. Everything is fine here." She didn't mention the upcoming meeting. "Take care of your wife and baby."

"I will." He ended the call.

Reed and Brady came into the living room as Brady explained the plan. "You'll tell Nate to take the west entrance and to pull over near the swing sets so you can meet him in the playground area."

"He won't like that if there are other people around," Reed said.

"There's a picnic table off to the side. That's where you can take custody of the evidence. Let him know that's your only option." Brady's gaze was serious. "We want to be prepared for anything."

"Understood." Reed moved away to use his phone. From what she could hear, it seemed his partner was happy enough to go along with the plan.

As they drove to Greenland Park, she sat in the back seat, twisting her hands together. Despite Brady's assurances, she was still worried.

But all she could do now was put her trust and faith in God's hands.

WHEN BRADY PULLED over at the side of the road on the opposite side of the swing set–designated meeting place, Reed glanced at him in surprise. "We're walking in from here?"

"Yes. I want to keep this vehicle hidden from view." Brady threw the gearshift into park and killed the engine. The three federal agents had met briefly so that Brady could get an earpiece and radio. Reed had balked at having one, knowing Nate would be suspicious. "I know you think all of these precautions are overkill, but I'd rather be prepared for the worst."

"I understand." Considering three cops were dead, he could agree Brady's precautions were not unreasonable.

"I'm going to hang back, hiding in the trees over there." Brady gestured with his hand. "Alanna promised to wait in the car. You'll do the meeting alone, but you need to let us know with a hand signal if something seems off. Between the three of us, we hope to stay on top of things, but since you don't have a radio, you'll need to let us know another way."

"I'll use a peace sign." Reed knew he could manage that much with his injured arm.

"Okay, let's do this." Brady pushed out of the vehicle. Reed opened his door, but Alanna's voice stopped him.

"Please be careful."

He glanced back at her. "I will. You stay safe, too, understand?"

"Yes, but you're the one walking into danger." She lifted her phone. "My orders are to call 911 if anything goes wrong."

"We'll be fine." He wanted desperately to kiss her but settled for a warm smile instead. "I'll be back before you know it."

"You better." Her attempt to look threatening was cute.

Shaking off her concern, he slid from the SUV and shut the door. The cool October breeze made him hope there weren't too many families or kids hanging around nearby. Not that he expected anything to go wrong, but as he walked across the dewy grass, he was relieved to note the playground area was vacant.

He scanned the area, taking note of the picnic table

Brady had mentioned. It was tucked beneath a large maple tree with leaves turning from green to yellow. Keeping his stance casual, he glanced around but couldn't see any sign of Brady, Doug, or Marc.

Not that he'd expected to.

The throbbing in his arm was no better, and he hadn't wanted to tell Alanna that he was feeling chilled. If she suspected he had a fever, she'd send him to the hospital faster than he could blink. He longed to sit at the picnic table but remained standing just in case.

He was letting the feds' paranoia mess with his brain.

Reed was doing this to help clear his name. If the feds figured out who was behind this, he wouldn't need it.

But if they didn't? Reed knew it was only a matter of time until a warrant was issued for his arrest.

He shifted from one foot to the other, searching for a sign of Nate's low-slung sports car, a black Corvette. A sweet ride like that would stick out here at the park like a sore thumb.

As the seconds ticked by, he was assailed by doubts. What if there already was a warrant issued for his arrest? Maybe Nate would lead other officers here to take him into custody.

He didn't want to believe his former partner would stoop to that level, yet Reed hadn't seen much of Nate since he'd stood up as best man at Nate's wedding.

A four-door blue sedan rolled to a stop on the opposite side of the playground from where Brady had parked the SUV. Since Reed had told Nate to use the west entrance, he had to assume the sedan belonged to Nate. Maybe it was his wife's car.

More likely, Wendy had forced him to sell the Corvette for something more reasonable.

Reed relaxed when Nate slid out from behind the wheel, then opened the back door to pull out a large box. It took a moment for his former partner to notice him standing near the picnic table. Nate quickly averted his gaze, shifting the box in his arms so he could close the back door.

A tingle of alarm settled at the base of his neck. He didn't make the peace sign, but it was obvious his former partner was uneasy.

Did Nate believe he was a dirty cop? That the evidence wasn't planted after all? No, that didn't make any sense. If so, Nate wouldn't bother to meet with him here. He'd have left the evidence wherever it was stashed in his house.

Nate carried the box toward him, his expression impassive. Reed purposefully stayed where he was, forcing his former partner to come to him.

"Hey, Nate, thanks for coming."

"Yeah, sure." Nate didn't smile in greeting. The tingle along the back of his neck morphed into a full-blown chill.

Something was off.

Keeping his stance casual, he rested his right hand on the butt of his gun. With his injured left arm, he lifted his hand and got ready to make the peace sign.

"You owe me for this," Nate said as he moved closer. "I wish you'd never contacted me. What if IAB had eyes on your place?"

Reed lowered his left hand without making the signal, thinking he'd overreacted. "Why would IAB have eyes on my house? I was cleared of killing Wesley with the video of two perps in hoodies stashing his body in the squad."

"Just leave me out of this next time," Nate groused as he dropped the box on the picnic table. "I have Wendy to think about."

In a flash, Nate pulled his weapon, pointing it at his

chest. Reed wished he'd made the peace sign but hoped that one of the feds would be able to see the gun.

If it wasn't covered by the box.

"What's going on, Nate?" Reed held his hands out, palms forward, as if that would calm down his former partner. The one guy he'd considered his closest friend. "What's with pulling a gun on me?"

"I've been told to bring you in. So let's go." Nate waved the tip of his weapon toward his blue sedan. Reed figured it must be an unmarked police car.

"On whose orders?" Reed stayed where he was. "Let me guess, Captain Jake Adams."

Nate's gaze flickered. "Yeah, so? You get an order from a captain, you follow through."

"He's playing you, Nate," Reed said. "He's the one who hid the drugs and cash in my house. He's the bad guy here, not me."

"Doesn't matter. Wendy is pregnant, and I'm up for a promotion." Nate shrugged. "This is your battle to fight, not mine. I'm just following orders. If you think I'm going to jeopardize my career for you, you're wrong."

Reed realized he'd been wrong about a lot of things. Nate's betrayal hit hard, although hearing about Wendy's pregnancy took some of the edge off.

One thing he'd learned from the Finnegans was family loyalty.

"Okay, that's fine. I'll go with you." He eased a step away from the picnic table so he'd have room to maneuver if needed. "How did Adams know about our conversation? Did you tell him?"

A commotion from the trees behind him snagged Nate's attention. Reed took advantage of the distraction by grabbing the box and throwing it toward his former partner. Unfortunately, the box was light.

Too light. As if there was nothing inside.

Nate fired his weapon, thankfully missing Reed as Marc Callahan and Brady Finnegan came darting out of the woods from two different directions.

"FBI! Drop your weapon! Now!"

"Feds?" Nate's eyes widened, and he immediately dropped his gun, raising his hands over his head. "You brought federal agents to the meeting?"

"Yes. And what did you bring, Nate?" Reed crossed over to retrieve the box. When he opened the flaps, he wasn't surprised to find it was empty. "Nothing."

A flash of movement caught his eye. When the door of the back seat of the sedan opened, he shouted, "Gun!"

Brady and Marc hit the ground, rolling to cover both threats—the person in the vehicle and Nate. Brady was closest to his former partner and managed to grab his ankle before he could escape.

Gunfire rang out. Reed crouched behind the picnic table, which didn't provide as much cover as he'd like, and returned fire.

"Who's in the car, Nate?" Reed shouted.

There was no answer. The abrupt silence that fell across the area was somehow louder than the gunfire.

Reed gingerly stood, trying to get a better view of the sedan. There was another burst of gunfire, but this time it came from the woods behind him.

A person fell out of the car, much the way his rookie partner had. Reed's eyes widened in surprise when he realized the cop was his buddy, Geoff Watkins.

How was it possible he had no friends in the force?

"Shooter is down," Doug shouted. "I've got one perp in cuffs."

"I've got Nate Jackson," Brady added.

"Anyone hit?" Reed asked. He glanced at his injured arm, grimacing at the blood that had seeped through Alanna's dressing.

"Just a nick," Brady responded.

Reed swallowed a groan, knowing Alanna would be upset about her brother getting hurt. Not that he blamed her.

This mess was his fault. He'd trusted his friends.

But they'd turned on him, in the worst way possible.

He straightened as Doug emerged from the trees dragging someone with him. Reed felt sick to his stomach when he saw Olivia Baker's wrists tied together with flexicuffs. Sheer animosity shone in her eyes.

"You ruined everything, Reed," she hissed.

He glanced from Olivia to Doug. "What happened?"

"I caught her sneaking through the woods to come up behind you." Doug sighed. "I tried to wait to take her down but didn't want to risk her shooting you, especially when I saw the gun in her hand."

Reed nodded, stunned to see the two people he'd trusted standing in the clearing. "Are you all working for Adams? Did he convince each of you that I was the dirty cop?"

A flicker of surprise darted across Olivia's features as Nate looked at her to answer. In that moment, he knew.

Olivia was the one working with Jake Adams. And she'd used his closest cop friends as pawns to get to him.

CHAPTER FIFTEEN

At the first sound of gunfire, Alanna called 911, then pushed out of the SUV. She wasn't foolish enough to run directly into a gun fight, but she crouched and ran to the nearest tree. If someone was hurt, she wanted to be ready.

Not Brady, Reed, or anyone helping them. Please, Lord? Her silent plea echoed over and over in her mind as she peered through the colorful foliage to see what was happening.

The abrupt silence that followed the staccato shots was unnerving. She couldn't see much from her position, so she edged closer, using the trees for cover.

When she heard Reed ask if anyone was hit, and Brady's response, she turned and ran to the SUV for the first aid kit. Then she darted through the trees to the clearing.

The first thing she noticed was the bright-red blood staining Reed's arm dressing. Then she swept her gaze over the area to see there were two people in cuffs. A man and a woman.

She'd never seen the man before in her life, but from the

angry expression on Reed's face, she presumed he did. The woman was the one they'd seen in the photograph with his deceased rookie partner.

Brady was over near a sedan checking the man lying on the ground. He shook his head as he stood, indicating there was nothing more to do. Since she knew her brother was fully capable of checking for a pulse—she'd taught him herself, after all—she didn't go over to investigate further.

"Your wound is bleeding." She set her giant first aid kit on the picnic table near Reed. There was a large cardboard box there, too, but it was empty.

She stared at the man Marc Callahan held in cuffs, realizing he must be Nate Jackson and that he'd betrayed Reed. Scumbag. Clearing her throat, she gestured to Reed. "I need to patch you up."

"Brady first." Reed nodded toward her brother.

"What?" She stepped forward, raking her gaze over her brother who'd rejoined them near the clearing. "You were hit?"

"I'm fine. A bullet pinged off a rock and hit me in the leg." He gestured to the dark stain on his lower calf. "The slug only grazed me."

Another wound with the high probability of infection. Alanna turned back to Reed. She reached out to take his hand, then scowled at the heat radiating from him. "You have a fever!" Her tone came out accusatory, as if he'd gotten his wound infected on purpose.

"Maybe." He brushed off her concern. "But the bigger issue is whether or not either of these disgraced cops are willing to rat out Captain Adams to save their own skin."

"You're the dirty cop," Nate said harshly. "Why did you do it, Reed? Money?"

"No, Adams is the dirty cop, and yeah, he's absolutely in

it for the money." Reed glanced at the woman standing beside Doug Bridges. "And Olivia is in on it too."

"I don't know what you're talking about." Olivia scowled. "You're the one we were trying to apprehend."

"Yeah, and got Geoff killed because of your efforts," Reed shot back. "Don't you think it's odd that Adams would send you here without backup?" He spread his uninjured arm wide. "While I have three federal agents supporting me?"

That was enough to convince Nate. He turned to glare at Olivia. "You did this? You lied to me?" When she didn't answer, he let out a sound of disgust. "I'll tell you everything you need to know, Reed. I thought I was helping by bringing you in. She told me this was an undercover op sanctioned by Adams. And that she needed me to get to you."

"And you didn't question it." Reed shook his head in disgust. "Geoff paid the ultimate price for your stupidity."

Another man had needlessly lost his life, and she prayed this was the end. Yet even as awful as this was, Alanna was grateful that God had watched over them.

Wailing police sirens filled the air. Backup was on the way, and she hoped this would be the end of the danger. That they'd nail Adams for his role in this.

"Both Brady and Reed need to go to the hospital." This time, she wasn't taking no for an answer. "The bullet that grazed Brady struck the rocky ground, so he'll need antibiotics. And it's clear the oral meds Reed has been taking aren't strong enough."

"That's fine." Marc flashed a grim smile. "We'll be working with these suspects to get more information on Jake Adams. I'm calling this in now. Based on what went down here, our SAC will issue an arrest warrant for Adams."

A flash of uncertainty darkened Olivia's features at his comment. Alanna wasn't the least bit surprised when the woman blurted, "I'll tell you everything I know. But you'd better hurry. Jake is heading to Mexico; the Blood Kings leader has a boss there. I—was supposed to join him when we'd finished here."

Conniving witch, Alanna thought. Finnegans didn't swear, but if there was ever an occasion that called for it, this was it.

It took far longer than she liked for the Greenland cops to get their statements. She finally sent Marc a pleading look, and he nodded, agreeing it was okay for her to take Brady and Reed to the emergency department at Trinity Medical Center.

Both men argued of course, but she ignored them. "Sepsis kills. You're going in, end of story."

Thankfully, they'd given up and gone along with her plan.

When they reached Trinity Medical Center, both men were taken directly into rooms. Reed's condition was more serious, and the staff didn't hesitate to insert an IV catheter to start fluids, followed by a dose of stronger antibiotics infused directly into his blood stream.

Alanna stood for a moment, holding Reed's hand. He was shivering, so she pulled the blanket up to his neck. "You'll feel better once the antibiotics are in."

"I can't believe Geoff is dead. And that Nate betrayed me." Reed's gaze was full of regret. "I thought they were my friends. Olivia too."

"I'm sorry, Reed. It's awful that things had to end up this way." She hated seeing him look so defeated.

"It's not over until Adams has been arrested," Reed

muttered. He gingerly shifted on the bed. "I'm fine, go check on your brother."

She didn't want to leave him. Not now, and not ever. But she nodded, thinking he might need some space to grieve in private. "I'll be back soon, okay?"

"Sure." His eyelids drifted closed.

She slid her hand from his, then turned to search for Brady. His room was located in the yellow team area. A step down from Reed's Orange team.

It could be worse, she reminded herself. They could have ended up in the red team. Or dead.

Brady was on the phone when she came in. She rolled her eyes, pointing to the sign that discouraged cell phone use. He ignored her. "Thanks, Marc. We'll let Reed know."

"Know what?" She moved closer, taking note of the bandage on his lower leg. Her brother also had IV fluids going, and she knew he'd get a dose of IV antibiotics too. "Did they find Adams?"

"They caught him at General Mitchell Airport." Brady grinned. "Kyleigh and another deputy helped grab him."

She nodded, knowing her sheriff's deputy sister was doing her six-month rotation at the airport. "I'm glad."

"Me too." Brady let out a heavy sigh. "Reed was right, Adams came from Chicago, his younger brother is a cop there. They're looking into him, too, as far as gang connections. There's still work to do as far as gathering evidence that will irrevocably nail his hide to the wall, but the good news is that he can't hurt anyone ever again."

"He's already cost the lives of so many." She rested her hand on her brother's arm. "Thanks for everything. Without your support, I'm not sure Marc and Doug would have been so willing to help."

"Trust me, they would. It was a team effort." Brady

grinned. "Let's take the win. By the way, I just spoke to Rhy. Devon is being discharged today, but not until this afternoon. He's heading down here to check on us. Mostly you."

"I'm glad to hear Devon is okay, but you should have assured Rhy there was no reason to come down."

"He wouldn't listen anyway." Brady waved a hand. "You know Rhy."

"True." Since there was nothing more for her to do here, she gave Brady a sisterly kiss on the cheek. "Behave and follow doctor's orders. I'm going to let Reed know the good news about Adams."

"You do that." Brady's eyes twinkled. "I suspect we'll be seeing more of him over the next few weeks."

She rolled her eyes without answering. She wasn't sure how Reed felt about that, and since the poor guy was battling a serious infection, this wasn't the time to discuss their future. If they even had one.

Turning, she headed back to the orange team. Faye wasn't on duty, but Dana Callahan was there, talking with one of the physicians. She noticed Karin Graves staring at her, then the housekeeper surprised her by gesturing for Alanna to come over.

She frowned and crossed over, following Karin as the housekeeper buzzed into the staff locker room. It took a moment for her to realize the young woman shouldn't have access to the space. Her locker was down in the house-keeping area, and the locker room wasn't cleaned during the day. Only on night shift.

The moment the door closed behind them, Karin abruptly turned, holding a small gun in her hand. Alanna blinked in confusion. "What are you doing?"

"You deserve to die." The young woman's fierce gaze

bored into her. Alanna didn't understand until she saw the plastic hospital ID badge in the woman's hand.

Her badge.

"It was you." Realization dawned. "You leaked my name to the reporters."

"Yes. Because you deserve to die!" Her voice rose. "He's dead because of you! My baby will never know his father because of you!"

"You're pregnant?" Alanna glanced down, belatedly noticing Karin's rounded belly. "With Ivan Garcia's baby?"

"Shut up." Karin lifted the gun higher. "He'd want me to finish what he started. The night you killed him."

"Don't do this." Alanna held her hands out in a pleading gesture, even though she realized the woman was likely beyond reason. "You'll end up having your baby in prison. Please, Karin, don't do this!" Alanna tried to project her voice loud enough to be heard beyond the locker room. Not that she held out much hope considering how busy the ED was. "My brothers are cops. You'll never get away with this. They'll find and arrest you!"

There was a buzzing sound as someone used their ID badge to enter the room. Karin's gaze darted toward the sound. Alanna didn't hesitate to lunge toward the woman, smacking the hand holding the gun with every ounce of strength she could muster. The gun spiraled out of Karin's hand, hitting the floor.

"No!" Karin screamed in pain and frustration as Alanna's weight forced her backward into the hard metal lockers.

"What's going on?" Dana Callahan gaped in surprise, then quickly stepped forward to help hold Karin down. "What did she do?"

"Gun." Her voice came out as a high squeak. She tried

again, willing her heart to settle down. "She pulled a gun on me. It's over there, on the floor."

"Why?" Dana asked.

"Garcia." Alanna pulled back from Karin but continued to hold the woman's arm in a tight grip. "She's pregnant with his child."

"Lord have mercy," Dana whispered. Alanna wasn't sure if she was praying for Karin or the baby. "Do you have her? I'll get security."

"Yeah." Alanna held Karin's wrist firmly, then grabbed the other, pulling it behind her back. She didn't have handcuffs but held both wrists so tightly the woman cried out with pain.

"You're hurting me," Karin whimpered.

"Not as badly as you were going to hurt me." Alanna still couldn't believe this young woman had picked up her badge and leaked her information to the press. For all she knew, her information from the ID badge had been used by Adams.

No wonder she and Reed had been found at her condo so quickly.

It only took a minute for security to arrive. Calvin wasn't on duty, but the two officers who'd responded gaped in shock when they'd heard about the gun Karin had used to threaten her.

"How did she get the gun past the metal detectors?" Sam asked as he snapped flexicuffs around Karin's wrists.

"You guys don't scan the employees," Dana pointed out. "Just patients and visitors."

"We'd better change that practice," Sam muttered. Karin had begun to sob quietly. Alanna couldn't help feeling sorry for her.

For the baby who would likely grow up without either parent.

"What's going on in here?" Her brother Rhy scowled from the open doorway.

"I'm fine. We're all fine." She brushed past security to join her brother. She hugged him, then stepped back. "Come with me to Reed's room. I'll explain everything to both of you."

The danger was over. For good, this time.

REED HATED feeling weak and helpless, but he was grateful for the antibiotics dripping into his veins. Anything that would help him feel better was a plus.

When he'd heard the commotion going on outside his door, he ignored it until he heard someone shout Alanna's name. He sat up, the room spinning for a moment. He stood, ignoring the way his hospital gown gaped open in the back showing off his navy-blue boxers, and grabbed the IV pole to steady himself. He quickly unplugged the machine, then wheeled it out to see what was going on. When the EKG wires held him back, he roughly ripped them off, sending the monitor over his bed beeping in protest.

"Alanna!" He swept his gaze over the group of employees gathered in one corner of the unit. "Alanna!" His heart thudded in his chest. What happened? What was going on?

"She's fine." A deep male voice snagged his attention. He relaxed when he saw Rhy walking toward him with Alanna at his side. She looked pale, so maybe she wasn't as fine as her brother seemed to believe.

"You shouldn't be up," Alanna scolded, reaching for his arm. "Let's get you back to bed."

"You're not hurt?" He didn't see any blood, but that didn't mean she wasn't injured.

"Karin the housekeeper stole my ID badge and leaked my name to the press." Alanna spoke quickly, trying to push him toward his room. "She threatened me with a gun because she's carrying Ivan Garcia's baby and blames me for his death."

"A gun?" His gaze clashed with Rhy's. Her older brother did not look happy.

"Don't worry, Dana must have sensed something was wrong. She came into the locker room, distracting Karin long enough for me to disarm her." Alanna's smile didn't quite reach her eyes.

He'd totally forgotten about the leaked information to the press. But it all made sense now that he knew the house-keeper was pregnant with Garcia's baby. He reluctantly allowed Alanna to escort him back to his room. "She should have held me responsible. I'm the one who shot him."

"It doesn't matter." Alanna sighed. "She'll pay for her crimes. And I'm more worried about her baby. An innocent child doesn't deserve this."

Reed knew what she meant. He swung himself back into bed. Alanna quickly reconnected the EKG patches. "You need to rest. By the way, Brady heard from Marc that Adams was arrested at the airport." She glanced at Rhy. "Kyleigh helped bring him in."

"That's good to hear." Rhy sighed and raked his hand through his hair. "I'm getting too old for this."

"Not true. Wait until your baby is a teenager." Reed had to smile when Alanna patted her brother's shoulder. "You'll really feel old then."

"Gee, thanks." Rhy met Reed's gaze. "And thank you for protecting my sister."

"Anytime." Reed gave Rhy a nod, then glanced at Alanna. Now that the nightmare was over, he wanted to speak with her.

Alone.

Rhy got the message. "I'll go check on Brady. Glad you're doing okay, Carmichael."

Alanna stepped closer, taking his hand. "You don't feel as feverish."

"I'm fine." He searched her gaze. "Before the night Ivan Garcia took you hostage, I was trying to find a good time to ask you out. You know, on a date."

She smiled. "I would have said yes."

"You would?" He lifted her hand to place it over his heart. "In that case, will you have dinner with me? Tonight? After I've been discharged?"

Her brow levered upward. "They might keep you overnight." She surprised him by leaning over to kiss him. "There's no rush, Reed. We can spend time together after you're healed."

"I don't want to wait that long." He tried not to sound like a whiny kid. "I don't need full use of my arm to take you out for dinner."

"Okay." She offered a hesitant smile. "But I could also cook for you. I'm not half bad."

"I love you." The words popped out before he could stop them. This wasn't the ideal place or time to tell her, but the way her eyes widened, he was glad he had. "I love you. And I hope you'll give me the chance to show you how much you mean to me."

A flash of uncertainty darkened her gaze. "Is this because your friends betrayed you? Because I promise I'm not going anywhere. I'll always be here to support you, no matter what. My family too."

He took a moment to search his feelings. "I can't lie, discovering how my friends believed the worst hurts. A lot. Yet Nate and Geoff thought they were following Captain Adam's orders. Olivia is the one who truly betrayed me." He paused, then added, "So to answer your question, no. My feelings for you have nothing to do with them. You're the one for me. I know I'm probably rushing things, and the last thing I want to do is to make you uncomfortable. But I wanted you to know how much I love you."

"Oh, Reed." Her smile widened, her deep-brown eyes shining with happiness. "I love you too."

"Really?" He truly hadn't expected her to reciprocate his feelings. "Okay, now I am feeling guilty for rushing things. Just agree to have dinner with me, and we'll take it from there."

Her warm chuckle washed over him. Despite being stuck in a hospital bed with IV antibiotics infusing in his arm, he was happy. "Yes, Reed. I'll have dinner with you."

"Did you mention that he'll have to attend family dinner on Sunday?" Brady asked from the doorway.

Reed glanced over in surprise. "How come you can get up and walk around, but I can't?"

"Don't be a pain, Brady." Alanna frowned. "There's plenty of time for Reed to run the gauntlet of Finnegan teasing."

"Not if he's professing his love for you." Brady eyed him speculatively. "We'll have to come up with a suitable nickname."

"Devon, Joy, Sami, Grace, and Faye don't have nick-names," Alanna said. "Why are you picking on us girls and the men we care about?"

"Because we can." Brady winked. "I just wanted to update you on the case. Adams isn't talking, but Marc says they found his disposable phone with texts and calls to the three cops who showed up on scene today, as well as several members of the Blood Kings. Doug is convinced Adams is going down, and hard, and Reed's former partner is cooperating fully with the investigation. We did good work today."

"Yeah, we did." It still bothered him to lose Geoff, not to mention the other cops who were caught in the line of fire. His rookie partner, Wesley Durango, Tate Brown, and Doyle Ford had paid the ultimate price. He'd tried to hold on to his faith and not question God's plan, but it wasn't easy. Still, there was some satisfaction in tossing a dirty cop in jail. Especially knowing Jake Adams would face the same fate he'd feared for himself. Maybe Adams would decide to cooperate to avoid being in jail with anyone from the Blood Kings. At this point, he didn't care as long as the rest of the good cops on the force were safe. He focused on Brady. "Thanks for letting us know."

"Anytime. Oh, and miraculously after Adam's arrest, there's no longer a bounty on your head. Chief Arnold Tanner held a press conference, vowing to relentlessly find and prosecute to the fullest extent of the law anyone who dared shoot at a cop."

"That's the way it should always be," Alanna said with a huff.

"I know. But we're certain the bounty on Reed's head was put out there by Adams himself, through his connections with the Blood Kings." Brady's expression turned serious. "I'm glad you're not hurt worse, Reed. The Finnegan clan owes you for saving Alanna's life."

"You can repay him by not giving him some silly nickname," Alanna shot back.

"Maybe we'll call him Superman. You know, because he flew to your rescue." Brady looked thoughtful for a moment, before turning away. "Don't worry, we'll come up with something. Take care, Reed. Alanna."

"Superman isn't terrible," he mused after Brady left.

"Trust me, they won't be that nice." Alanna scowled. "They dubbed Bax Scala, Kyleigh's husband, Penguin just because he's rich enough to own a tux and wore one to Rhy and Devon's wedding. He was the only one in formal wear, and the guys were relentless. Thankfully, Bax took it in stride and doesn't seem to care."

"Hey." He brushed a kiss over her knuckles. "I love your family, and I don't give a rip about a silly nickname either. I have an older brother, too, remember? All I care about is you."

"That's sweet, Reed." She shook her head with a rueful smile. "I think you might be the one guy who isn't intimidated by my brothers."

"Not in a million years. I respect them. And I can't wait to meet the rest of your family."

"Be careful what you wish for," she teased. Then she bent over to kiss him again. This time, he pulled her close, kissing her deeply. He loved her so much.

She broke off the embrace, glancing up when his IV began to beep. "Your antibiotic is finished."

"Good, maybe they'll cut me loose too." He caught her hand. "I have a very important date with a beautiful nurse."

"You'll stay as long as they tell you to, understand?" She held his gaze. "For me?"

"Only for you," he agreed. He wanted to be back at full strength too. Because the entire world was brighter now that he could bask in the warm glow of Alanna's love.

EPILOGUE

Three weeks later . . .

Alanna was relieved Reed had been given the okay to begin strength training in his injured arm. His plan of leaving the hospital the same day as Brady had not happened. He'd ended up getting five days of IV antibiotics to fight the infection that had festered in his wound. She couldn't quite shake the guilt knowing she was the one who'd removed the bullet and hadn't forced him to go in for proper treatment.

Reed had pointed out that everything had happened for a reason. They'd gotten Adams, and that was the most important thing of all. Apparently, Adams's brother, the Chicago cop, was also involved in getting money from the gangs in return for protection. Both cops had been arrested and were being held without bail.

Karin Graves had pled guilty to menacing with a deadly weapon, a far cry from the attempted murder charge Maddy Callahan had initially slapped on her. Karin lost her job at the hospital for bringing a gun to work and for her felony conviction. Alanna decided maybe it was okay that the young woman had taken the lesser charge, for the baby's sake.

Her buzzer rang, startling her from her thoughts. Even though she knew Reed was due any second, she answered, "Yes, who is it?"

"Your hot boyfriend." Reed's chuckle made her smile.

"Come on up." She shook her head at his antics. Despite being wounded and losing so many of his friends, Reed had found solace in attending church with the Finnegan family. She was thrilled at how he'd attended Bible study with her too.

"Hey, beautiful." Reed pulled her in for a kiss. "Ready to go?"

"The bigger question is whether you're ready to face the family." This Sunday, everyone except Faye and Sami had the day off, a very rare occurrence.

He puffed out his chest in a comical imitation of Superman. "I'm ready."

"Goof." She pulled on her denim jacket in deference to the chill in the late October air and followed him down to the first-floor lobby. She wasn't concerned about Reed fitting in. Rhy, Brady, Tarin, and Aiden had already gotten to know him.

The drive to the Finnegan homestead didn't take long. The driveway was already full of cars, so Reed parked on the street. They entered the house without needing to use the security system since there were so many cops with guns inside.

"Clark, it's good to see you." Aiden clapped him on the shoulder, taking care to avoid his injured side.

"Lois and I wouldn't miss it." The Superman moniker had stuck, but they'd all taken to calling him Clark in honor of Clark Kent. She rolled her eyes at her twin.

"I have no idea why I put up with you guys," she muttered.

"Because you love us." Aiden gestured toward the dining room. "Go on in. Elly claims the pot roast is ready; we can eat any time."

"Sound good, I'm hungry." Reed took her hand in his as they crossed the kitchen and living area to the large dining room. The place was packed with Finnegans and their spouses.

"Oh great, you're here!" Elly smiled. "Please sit down, I'll bring everything in shortly."

"I hope there's enough food for all of us," Aiden joked with a mock serious expression. "Otherwise, someone's likely to get stabbed with a fork."

"Not me," Colin swiftly interjected. "It's my turn to stab you."

"You can try," Aiden said. "But I might get you first."

Reed arched a questioning brow, and she nodded. "Yeah, they're not kidding."

"Harsh crowd. Remind me not to get between them and their food," Reed muttered. Then he stopped at the end of the table. "I—uh, would like to have everyone's attention, please."

Alanna wasn't sure what Reed wanted to say, but everyone in her family had an expectant look on their face.

Everyone except Rhy.

"I want you all to know how much I love Alanna." Reed turned, then dropped to one knee. Elly gasped when he pulled out a small velvet box. "Alanna, will you please marry me?"

She couldn't believe he'd asked her here in front of everyone. But then she understood he'd already asked Rhy for permission to marry her. The same way he would have asked her father if their parents were still alive. Tears pricked her eyes. "Yes, Reed. I'd be honored to marry you."

"Yay," Elly cried. She grabbed a napkin off the table and dabbed her eyes. "That was the most romantic proposal yet."

Reed held her gaze as he opened the ring box and produced a diamond ring. "If you don't like this, we'll get something else."

"I love it. But I love you more." The diamond glittered on her finger, and a second later, he'd scooped her into his arms.

"Thank you for making me the happiest man in the world," he whispered in her ear.

"Ditto," she whispered back, then laughed when he spun her in a circle.

"Hey, enough celebrating already, Clark," Quinn complained. "I'm hungry. It's time to eat."

Reed burst out laughing, not the least bit annoyed at the interruption. He kissed her and then gestured to the table. "After you."

She caught Rhy's gaze seeing frank approval reflected there. In that moment, she knew without a shred of doubt Reed would be a wonderful addition to their family.

And she couldn't wait until they could make it official.

I HOPE you enjoyed Alanna and Reed's story in *Critical Response*. Are you ready to read Aiden and Shelby's story in *Strategic Threat*? Click Here!

DEAR READER

I hope you are enjoying my Finnegan First Responder series. I'm loving how the Finnegan siblings have been falling in love while dodging danger. I'm hard at work on Aiden's story, which will soon be followed by Elly's. I am super excited to write about the Christmas family reunion between the Finnegans and the Callahans in her book! I hope you like it too.

Anyone choosing to purchase e-books or audiobooks directly from my website will receive a 15% discount by using the code **LauraScott15**. I usually have the Finnegan books available there first, before they are released on other vendor sites.

I adore hearing from my readers! I can be found through my website at https://www.laurascottbooks.com, via Facebook at https://www.facebook.com/LauraScott Books, Instagram at https://www.instagram.com/laurascott books/, and Twitter https://twitter.com/laurascottbooks. Also, take a moment to sign up for my monthly newsletter to learn about my new book releases! All subscribers receive a free novella not available for purchase on any platform.

Until next time,
Laura Scott
PS Read on for a sneak peek of *Strategic Threat*.

STRATEGIC THREAT

Chapter One

Staff Sergeant Aiden Finnegan stood at ease dressed in his army dress blues. The cold November wind rattled the branches of the bare trees surrounding the Central Wisconsin Veterans Memorial Cemetery. He wasn't on duty today as a member of the Army National Guard. He'd come as a pallbearer and to pay his respects to his former commander, Sergeant Major Gregory Savage.

He surreptitiously watched the beautiful blond Shelby Copeland, née Savage, wipe at her tears while holding the hand of a young girl roughly three years old. He'd met Shelby before as he'd served with her husband, Emmitt Copeland, before he'd been killed in the line of duty.

The young mother had lost her husband two years ago and was now attending her father's funeral. His heart ached for her. She looked fragile, pale, and alone standing in the cold as the pastor spoke of her father's dedication and service to his country.

Difficult to comprehend the man he'd long admired was

dead. Sergeant Major Greg Savage had prided himself in staying in top physical condition. Even at the age of fifty-eight, the officer could keep up with the younger soldiers in his command. He and the other five soldiers chosen to carry the commander's casket struggled to understand how their sergeant major could have died of a sudden heart attack.

Yet here they were, burying the man with full military honors near his hometown of Oshkosh, Wisconsin.

When the pastor finished his brief sermon, Aiden allowed his gaze to roam over the oddly small group gathered at the gravesite. He'd expected more attendees for a high-ranking sergeant major like Greg Savage. Yet some in the military deemed the National Guard to be less important than the regular army, navy, air force, and marines. Oh, and the Coast Guard. The National Guard was not considered nearly as important. He watched as the bugler stepped forward, lifting the horn to his mouth to begin playing taps. The twenty-one-gun salute and folding of the flag would follow.

His eyes lingered for a moment on Shelby and her daughter. What was the little girl's name? Eva? The last time he'd seen the girl she'd been a baby. Shelby appeared stoic and somber, but the little girl looked around curiously, likely too young to appreciate the solemn event. Then he snapped to attention as the soldier with the bugle began to play.

The familiar notes hit him hard, as they always did. The scene was reminiscent of Shelby's husband's funeral, although there had been more attendees back then. He kept his gaze focused on the ground near Shelby's and Eva's feet. Once he'd imagined dedicating his life to the military, climbing the ranks the way Savage had.

But lately he'd been considering a change. His current

tour of duty was nearly over, formally finished at the end of December. He'd originally planned to reenlist. Yet he hadn't signed the paperwork.

Maybe it was time to get out and search for a career with a regular schedule. The way most of his siblings were getting married, settling down, and having families made him keenly aware of his lack of social life. Frequent deployments made dating difficult. Maria had made it clear she was done waiting around for him. He couldn't blame her.

After the final notes from the bugle faded, seven soldiers stepped forward, rifles resting on their shoulders. It was time for the twenty-one-gun salute. He knew the seven soldiers would fire off three rounds. In choreographed unison, they lifted their weapons and fired into the sky.

Something kicked up a bit of the icy-hard ground inches from where Shelby stood. Aiden reacted without thinking, lunging forward and grabbing Shelby and her daughter with his arms and pulling them out of the way, using his own body for coverage.

The seven soldiers were already firing their second round before anyone seemed to realize what was going on.

"What are you doing?" Shelby gazed up at him shell-shocked.

"We need to get out of here! Now!" He ruthlessly pulled her up, then reached down to lift the crying toddler into his arms. "Hurry!"

The rest of the funeral attendees slowly began to rush forward. Thankfully, he had a head start. He pulled Shelby with him as he zigzagged through tombstones to cross the frozen ground toward the line of trees.

"Have you lost your mind? What's wrong with you?" Shelby demanded.

"A bullet hit the ground near your feet." He continued

moving through the foliage, sweeping his gaze around the area, searching for the gunman.

"It was probably from the soldiers' twenty-one-gun salute!" Shelby yanked against his grip. "Let me go, Aiden. You're being ridiculous."

He wasn't, so he ignored her. Once they reached the shelter of the trees, he turned to look at her. "I saw the frozen ground kick up under the impact of a bullet. Someone took a shot at you under the cover of the salute honoring your father. The trajectory was such that it couldn't possibly have been from the seven soldiers firing into the air during the twenty-one-gun salute."

Her eyes widened, and she finally stopped tugging against him. Ignoring Eva's crying wasn't easy. He could hear the ruckus behind him and knew the other pallbearer soldiers back at the gravesite were coming to find them.

He knew none of them could have fired the bullet he'd seen hit the ground, but that didn't mean one or more of them weren't involved.

As he'd anticipated, several of the funeral attendees caught up to them. He abruptly stopped, thrust Eva into Shelby's arms, and turned to face them. He lifted his hands to show he wasn't holding a weapon.

"Did any of you see the shooter?" he asked.

"What shooter?" Sergeant Oliver Kennedy asked. "What's wrong with you, Finnegan? Are you planning on holding Shelby and her daughter hostage?"

"No. I was getting them out of the way of the shooter." He outranked the soldier and did his best to level him with a stern glare. He didn't care if Oliver had been friends with Emmitt. "Go back to the gravesite. Inspect the ground where Shelby and Eva were standing. You'll see what I mean."

Kennedy exchanged glances with the others.

"I didn't see anything," Victor Morrison muttered.

"Fine. I'll go," Oliver agreed. "But these guys are staying here to make sure you haven't lost your mind and are planning something stupid."

His jaw tightened at his subordinate's comment, but he didn't respond. Behind him, Shelby was comforting her daughter, and Eva's crying turned into sniffles. He lowered his voice and said, "Please stay behind me, Shelby."

She didn't respond, but she didn't move away either. He was glad she was taking his concern seriously.

A long, uncomfortable silence stretched between them. Aiden knew what he'd seen, and he wasn't about to back down despite the group of men and women facing him.

It seemed like hours instead of minutes before Sergeant Kennedy returned, his expression grim. "I found the area in the ground that you mentioned, Finnegan. I found the slug. It's not the same ammo used in the twenty-one-gun salute."

The discovery did not fill him with relief. Just the opposite. He wasn't sure who had come to the sergeant major's funeral to kill Shelby or why. "I need you and the rest of the team to spread out and search the area for the shooter. He's likely long gone but may have left evidence behind."

"Yes, sir," Kennedy replied, although the way he glanced at Shelby indicated Oliver would rather stay there to help protect the young mother. Victor, too, didn't seem to like the idea of leaving.

"Oh, and let the pastor and the other funeral attendees know the service is over," he added. "I'm taking Ms. Copeland and her daughter home."

Shelby sputtered in protest. He turned to look at her. "Do you want to put your daughter in danger?"

She pressed her lips together and shook her head. "Of

course not. But there's no way that bullet was meant for me. Whoever fired it must have terrible aim."

"I disagree." To his mind, the bullet had come far too close. But her comment gave him pause. Soldiers were trained to hit what they were aiming at. So why had this shooter missed?

It didn't make sense. Especially because he went so far as to use the twenty-one-gun salute to cover the sound of his own weapon. Then again, maybe the guy had been too focused matching the timing of the rifles being fired, rather than making the perfect shot.

"Let's get out of here." He put his arm around Shelby's waist, urging her across the hard ground toward the road where he'd left his truck. He doubted the shooter had stuck around, but he wasn't taking any chances.

"I have my car here." Shelby subtly pulled away from him. "I'll drive myself home."

"Not happening." He had to bite back a flash of anger. Striving for patience, he added, "Please, Shelby. I don't want anything to happen to you or Eva."

"You're taking this whole army obligation to Emmitt a little too far, aren't you?"

Aiden doubted she'd appreciate how his knowing her deceased husband had nothing to do with his motives. In truth, Oliver Kennedy and Nolan Hanover were closer to Emmitt than he had been. "Emmitt would want me to look after you."

"Whatever." She suddenly sounded exhausted, as if the long funeral and the frantic rush from the burial had sapped her strength.

"I'll keep you and Eva safe." They reached the road where several of the funeral attendees were already in their respective cars intent on getting out of there as soon as possible.

One soldier glared at him as he passed, as if the abrupt ending to the solemn occasion was his fault. Aiden knew God had been watching over Shelby and her daughter today. He was just grateful he'd noticed the bullet striking the icy ground.

"We need to use my car," Shelby insisted when he paused near his cherry-red truck. "Eva's car seat is inside."

That hadn't occurred to him, although it should have. He'd taken Brady's son, Caleb, to the zoo twice and knew young kids needed to be in car seats.

"Fine. But I'm driving."

"I'm not in the military, Aiden, so stop ordering me around like I'm one of your soldiers," Shelby snapped.

He swallowed a retort and tried to soften his tone. "I'm sorry. The only reason I'd like to drive is to make sure we're not followed."

She sighed, then nodded. "You could have explained that up front. Clear communication goes a long way."

No argument there. Shelby led the way to a Jeep SUV, opening the back to help Eva get inside. He stood behind her, scanning the area for any sign of a threat. When she finished, he opened the passenger door for her. "Keys?"

"I have the fob in my purse." Clearly, she had no intention of giving it to him. He closed the door behind her, then jogged around to slide in behind the wheel. Seconds later, he pulled out onto the road and followed the trailing cars out of the cemetery.

"Do you have any idea why someone would do this?" He glanced over to where Shelby sat, twisting her hands in her lap. She was dressed in funeral black—her sweater, skirt, heeled pumps and coat. "Why you've been targeted?"

"No! I have no idea." Her raised voice was laced with fear. "This doesn't make any sense! I'm a teacher, not involved in the military like you and my father. I haven't done anything wrong. Why on earth would anyone shoot at me?"

It was a fair question. Too bad he had no answer.

SHELBY WANTED to cry but held herself together for Eva's sake. At first, she'd wanted to believe this was nothing but Aiden Finnegan's overactive imagination. But then Oliver claimed to have found a mark in the dirt and a bullet. One that was a different caliber than the one the soldiers carrying out the twenty-one-gun salute were using.

And worse? It had struck the ground near the exact location where she and Eva had been standing!

"Maybe the, uh, attempt was meant for someone else." She turned in her seat, offering a reassuring smile for her daughter. Eva was looking sleepy, no doubt tired from the long day too. The little girl probably didn't know what a bullet was, but she didn't like having this conversation in front of her three-year-old daughter.

"The pastor?" Aiden arched a brow. "Doubtful."

"Anything is possible." A theory she desperately wanted to believe. "Why not? Could be he has some dark secret past. I sure don't."

Aiden frowned but didn't reply. She could tell he wasn't sold on the idea. But the more she thought about the near miss, the more logical it was that she and Eva were just innocent bystanders.

Not specifically targeted by a gunman.

Staring down at her hands, she imagined she could still

see the indentation from her wedding ring. She'd taken it off six months after Emmitt's death but hadn't dipped her toe back in the dating pool.

She wasn't interested in starting over. Besides, teaching and taking care of Eva took all her time and energy. An energetic just-turned-three-year-old was both a blessing and exhausting. By the time Eva fell asleep, she was too tired to do anything else.

"Shelby?" Aiden's husky voice drew her gaze. "Are you okay?"

She shook her head but glanced pointedly back at Eva, indicating she didn't want to talk about it. He seemed to understand, and when he turned onto the highway, she noticed he'd headed toward Oshkosh. She pulled herself together, glad to know she'd be home soon. "I live off Sunset View Road, not far from the church."

"I remember." Aiden met her gaze. "I was there after Emmitt's funeral."

She glanced away. Sometimes it seemed as if Emmitt might walk in the door at any moment, coming home from a recent deployment. And other times she found it difficult to remember what it was like to be married. Their union had only lasted four years, and Eva had no memory of her father since he died just after her first birthday.

Aiden slowed and quickly moved into the right lane. She frowned, as this wasn't their exit. The way he kept his gaze on the rearview mirror made her stomach tighten. "Something wrong?"

"No."

The tense expression on his face belied his response. Twisting in her seat, she scanned the traffic behind her. He was driving at the speed limit, and car after car zoomed by, passing them on the left.

Was he doing this just to make her paranoid? Her gaze lingered on her sleeping daughter for a moment, then she sat back with a frown. Emmitt had said Aiden was decent guy. But other than meeting Aiden a handful of times—yes, including during Emmitt's funeral—she didn't know much about him.

Other than he came from a large family with something like eight brothers and sisters. As an only child, she couldn't imagine having that many siblings.

She lurched in her seat when Aiden made an abrupt turn, exiting the interstate at the last possible second. Grabbing the hand rest with one hand, she braced herself on the dashboard with the other.

Before she could ask what he was doing, he hit the gas, flying through a yellow light that turned red the moment they reached the center of the intersection. Car horns blared, and a wave of anger hit hard. Eva was in the car! If they'd been hit, her daughter would be injured, or worse!

"What's wrong with you?" It was all she could do not to scream at him, but she did use her best stern-teacher voice, lowered so as not to wake Eva. "Pull over right now! I don't feel safe with you speeding like a maniac through yellow lights."

Aiden ignored her, weaving between cars before turning sharply and taking the on-ramp to get back on the interstate. Only they were going the wrong way.

She smacked him in the arm, her knuckles brushing against the stripes on his uniform sleeve. A quick glance back confirmed Eva was still asleep. "Why are you acting like this?"

"There was an SUV following us." His tense tone sent shivers down her spine. She twisted again in her seat but didn't see anything.

"Are you sure?"

"Yes." He shot her a concerned look. "The black SUV stayed in the middle lane but dropped his speed dramatically when I did. No one does that, Shelby. I had no choice but to bail."

She wasn't sure what to think. Her husband knew Aiden, along with several of the other men who'd been at the funeral today, so logically she should be able to trust him. But this—couldn't be happening. There was no reason for anyone to follow or shoot at her!

Unless . . .

Pressing a hand to her racing heart, she forced the question past her tight throat. "Do you think this is related to my father?"

"That possibility has occurred to me." Aiden didn't meet her gaze; his attention seemed to be riveted on the rearview mirror. "I don't understand what's going on here, but I don't think you should go home. Not yet."

She stared at him. "I have to go home. I have school next week." Today was Thursday, and she'd been given Friday off as a bereavement day. But her principal expected her to be in her classroom teaching fourth graders on Monday.

His jaw tightened. "I don't care. It's too risky."

She was getting mighty tired of him telling her what she could and couldn't do. Pulling herself together, she lifted her chin. "Isn't it possible that you're overreacting? Just because some guy slowed down on the interstate when you did doesn't mean he was following us. Maybe he assumed you saw a cop?" She crossed her arms over her chest. "Take us home. Now. Eva will need a snack soon."

As if on cue, her daughter spoke up. "Mommy? I'm hungry."

"We'll be home soon, sweetie." She glared at Aiden. "Right?"

He shook his head as if frustrated, but then he exited the freeway. This time, he didn't get back on the interstate. He stayed on a rural highway. She wanted to snap at him again but managed to hold her tongue.

Now that she was thinking more clearly, the idea of her father somehow causing danger to show up here at his funeral of all places didn't make sense either. He'd dedicated his life to serving the Army National Guard. He was approaching his thirty years of service and had been scheduled for another promotion.

Besides, the role of the National Guard was to protect the public and provide assistance during natural disasters. It was the one branch of the service where soldiers were responsible for protecting the United States rather than being sent abroad. That was hardly the sort of career that encouraged or supported criminal activity.

Aiden's stern features and long silence indicated he was angry. Too bad. So was she. This wasn't how she'd imagined her father's funeral would go.

"Mommy, I'm hungry!" Eva's insistent tone had her rummaging in her small purse for a bag of fish crackers.

"Here." She turned and gave the small baggie to her daughter. There would be orange cheese smears over everything back there, including Eva's face and hands, but she didn't care. "We'll be home soon. Right, Staff Sergeant Finnegan?"

He scowled. "Aiden. And yes, we'll be there soon."

Rubbing her temple, she let out a silent sigh. "I'm sorry," she murmured. "It's been a long day."

He shot her a surprised glance, then nodded. "I understand."

Seeing the church steeple up ahead, she estimated they were less than five minutes from her home. Her feet ached from her low-heeled pumps, more so after the mad dash across the cemetery to hide in the trees. She couldn't wait to get out of her funeral attire.

The thought of never seeing her father again hit hard. Not that he'd been around much when she was a kid, but later, after her mother had died, he'd done his best to balance his homelife with his career.

And after Emmitt had died, her dad had been her rock. Helping as much as he could with Eva between homeland deployments.

"You have off tomorrow?" Aiden's question caught her off guard.

"Yes. I was given five bereavement days to plan and attend his funeral." She shrugged. "It would be nice to be off longer, but the Thanksgiving break will be here before you know it. I didn't want to use any more personal days." Another pang hit hard at knowing her father wouldn't be there for his favorite holiday, Thanksgiving.

Or at the upcoming Christmas holiday either.

Aiden passed her street. "You missed the turn."

"I'm going around the block as an extra precaution," he told her. "Eva's okay with her crackers, right? A slight detour isn't going to hurt anything."

"I guess not." She wondered again if he was doing this on purpose just to scare her.

After circling the block, he headed down her street. As Aiden drove toward her house, a small brown ranch building with large trees on either side, she wondered how he planned to get home.

Then she told herself that was his problem, not hers.

As her vehicle slowed, she caught a glimpse of movement along the side of her house. A shadow beneath her tree. Dusk was falling, so she wasn't absolutely sure she hadn't imagined it.

Until she heard the crack of gunfire.

Aiden hit the gas, the Jeep lurching forward. She grabbed the hand rest again as they took a sharp turn, and Eva started crying.

Then Aiden punched the accelerator, speeding away from her normally quiet and serene neighborhood.

Stunned, she couldn't believe what had just happened.

Aiden had been right all along. Someone really had tried to kill her!